Firehole River Murder

Yellowstone Fly-Fishing Mystery Series

By

Raymond Kieft

authorHOUSE™

1663 LIBERTY DRIVE, SUITE 200
BLOOMINGTON, INDIANA 47403
(800) 839-8640
WWW.AUTHORHOUSE.COM

© 2004 Raymond Kieft.
All Rights Reserved.

No part of this book may be reproduced, stored in a retrieval system, or transmitted by any means without the written permission of the author.

First published by AuthorHouse 11/20/04

ISBN: 1-4184-6456-2 (sc)

Library of Congress Control Number: 2004097489

Printed in the United States of America
Bloomington, Indiana

This book is printed on acid-free paper.

Prologue
Wednesday
April 24, 1978

Daniel Strong sat in the driver's seat of the van feeling sick to his stomach. His hands were slippery on the steering wheel from the sweat that made his shirt stick to his back. Even though the air conditioning was going full blast, sweat beaded on his forehead, causing him to wipe his eyes with the sleeve of his shirt. What if something went wrong? Could these guys be trusted? After all, he didn't know either of them very well. But, what could go wrong? The plan had been gone over more than twenty times. The individual parts had been rehearsed at least ten times in the vacant Denver theater building and the parking lot behind it. While he didn't know very much about his two accomplices, he knew enough about the brains behind this caper that the two individuals presently inside the University of Colorado Health Sciences Center weren't amateurs. The mastermind, who had first contacted him and explained what he wanted, didn't hire amateurs. These guys had to know what they were doing. But as much as he tried to convince himself, the realization that the slightest error on the part of his two accomplices could blow the whole operation brought the nausea back to his stomach and the sweat to again bead on his forehead.

It hadn't taken much convincing by the mastermind to rope Daniel into this operation. He had been asked to drive the van from the Health Sciences Center to the vacant garage, where another person would be waiting with a car to take the stuff that his two accomplices were right now taking from Professor Boersma's laboratory in the Health Sciences Center. He had been promised $100,000 for his part in this caper. With this money, he would begin a new life in Las Vegas.

Another wave of nausea passed over him. Not the smartest way to ensure that he wouldn't spend the rest of his life in a federal penitentiary, relying on two guys he knew nothing about. Even the thought of spending a few weeks or months behind bars made his stomach ache worse. At age twenty-two, he was simply too young to be doing this type of stupid thing. He felt the urge to hit the accelerator and drive away, leaving the two yokels currently inside the Health Sciences Center to fend for themselves.

But the plans were foolproof, weren't they? And $100,000 for fifteen minutes' work, how could you beat that? He hadn't told anyone, not even Mr. Mastermind, about what he was going to do after he drove the van into that vacant garage. He had done a dry run a few nights ago. There was a Denver RTD bus stop a few blocks from the garage. Currently on the front seat of the van next to him was a change of clothes stuffed in a black garbage bag. He would change into those clothes, stuff the clothes he was wearing into the garbage bag, and dump the garbage bag in a dumpster that he had seen on the corner opposite the bus stop. He would wait for a bus and hop on the first one that came along. Thankfully, this bus route was heavily used, so buses arrived every few minutes. He had ridden buses from three different routes a few days ago, so he knew they all stopped near a motel where he planned to hole up for a few days and allow the police dragnet to pass. He had already paid for the motel room for a week with cash. After it appeared safe to leave, he would grab a taxi to Stapleton International Airport and fly to Las Vegas using a ticket he had purchased using a fictitious name.

Checking his watch, he realized that in two minutes, if everything went according to plan, his two accomplices would emerge from the Health Sciences Center with their satchels holding the highly toxic material taken from Professor Boersma's lab. The figure of $10 million as the value of the stuff had been mentioned in hushed conversation during a recent practice run. Mr. Mastermind had told him the Russian government was eager to obtain the stuff. Why it was headed to Russia and why the Russians would pay $10 million didn't make sense to him, but he wasn't being paid to have things like this make sense. Driving the van and transferring the toxic material to the contact person, who right now should be waiting inside the vacant garage, was all he needed to know and do. What happened to the stuff after he turned it over to the contact man was no business of his, and he frankly didn't care to know. The $100,000 would be wired to a bank account in Las Vegas under a false name different from the one on his airline ticket. The account had been opened six weeks earlier using a false ID and social security number, which a forger working for Mr. Mastermind had provided.

Checking his watch again, he saw it was thirty seconds to launch time. What was coming around the corner? A group of teeny boppers with their skateboards—jiving smack dab on the sidewalk that was the escape route from the Health Sciences Center to where he waited in the van. What should he do? Would he be able to warn his two accomplices to steer clear of the teenagers? It was too late to do anything as he saw the two men emerge from the Health Sciences Center. He watched as they tried to get through the group of teenagers to the van. One of the teenagers fell to the ground, being pushed out of the way. Staring in disbelief as bedlam broke out, he knew this meant nothing but trouble, big-time trouble. Abort the operation, he wanted to scream, but his voice was frozen. He felt he would vomit.

The two men finally made a break away from the teenagers and came running toward the van. Watching in horror as two of the teenagers took after the two men and tried to pull them down, Daniel would never forget what happened next. It was as if time stood still, and everything that happened, happened in slow motion. A shot was fired from close range, and one of the teenagers crumpled to the ground screaming. The other teen's eyes met Daniel's, and their eyes remained locked in a stare that seemed to last forever before Daniel broke away as the side door of the van flew open and the two men tumbled in shouting, "Go, go; let's get out of here."

He drove the van as fast as he could, tearing down the side streets too numb to comprehend what was being said behind him on the floor of the van. "Stupid punk," "Why'd you have to shoot him?" "Got to get rid of the gun," and "Is he dead?" registered with him as he drove the van into the vacant garage. His hands were shaking, and he felt like he would pass out at any time. What if the kid was dead? He would be an accomplice to a murder. All he could think about was the stare of the teenager, realizing that his face had been seen. Daniel Strong could be placed at the scene of the burglary, which might also involve a murder.

Chapter One
May 22, 2003
Friday

Talk about having mixed feelings. On the one hand, Parker Williams was elated with the $1,800 fly-fishing outing, which had been scheduled only a few minutes ago by his fly shop for six clients for tomorrow. On the other hand, one of the clients was a guy he wasn't keen on being around, let alone having to serve him as a fishing guide. But the money for one day's work was too good to pass up, so he had swallowed hard and acted enthusiastic when his employee, Jim Hill, told him about the telephone call that had led to scheduling the outing.

"I'm glad you took the call and not me," Parker had said. "I wasn't in the mood to talk with anyone."

"No problem. The guy calling said he knew you, and he wanted to schedule an outing for himself and five other people for fly-fishing in Yellowstone National Park," Jim had responded. "His name is Edgar Hickson. Said he is a university president. I have his phone number if you want to call him. He said he is staying at the Cutthroat Conference Center at Big Sky."

Parker had cringed when he heard the name Edgar Hickson. Edgar was one of those people you wished you would never see or talk to again after the first time you met or talked with him. Pompous, arrogant, a know-it-all attitude with a superior-than-thou view of himself summed up how Parker remembered Edgar Hickson. Not the kind of person you wanted to be around for very long. "Am I supposed to call him back," Parker had asked, "or did you work out the details so I don't have to call him back? Please tell me you did."

"He didn't say you had to call him back, but I suppose you can if you feel you want to," Jim had responded.

The reason Parker hadn't wanted to talk with anyone was that he had been experiencing some remorse related to the life-changing decision he had made that resulted in his now living in West Yellowstone, Montana, and owning a fly-fishing shop.

Only a little more than one year earlier, he had resigned his appointment as president of Sturbridge State University in Sturbridge, Massachusetts, and moved to West Yellowstone.

Fed up with the faculty union's acceptance of mediocrity as the standard for its members, he had resigned his appointment effective fifteen months earlier. The liberal politics of Massachusetts and the terrible tax load, which made people refer to the state as Taxachusetts, also contributed to his decision. The final blow had been the shock of his wife of two years walking out on him to take up with a faculty member from the university where he had previously served as academic vice president. With no children, he concluded that he needed a dramatic change in his life if he was to have any chance of living out his life with some happiness.

Jumping into the fly-shop business, let alone owning a shop, was the farthest thing from his mind when he first came to West Yellowstone. Getting away from university life and the memories of his former marriage, while immersing himself in the genuineness of a small community and the wholesomeness of its people, while pursuing his twin passions of fly-fishing and geology, had been his only desires. Because he had visited it several times on fishing trips and also to do research on the geological and thermal wonders of Yellowstone National Park, he felt West Yellowstone would be a genuine community where people accepted each other for who they were and were honest in their interpersonal relationships. Of course, it didn't hurt that it stood on the edge of the nation's flagship national park with its reputation as a fly-fishing mecca.

He had selected the name Gold Medal for the fly shop since a gold medal recognizes the best, and he intended this fly shop to be known for quality service and merchandise. His was one of five fly shops located in West Yellowstone, Montana, a town with a population of eight hundred year-round residents that grew to five thousand during the summer months. Centered in the middle of the best fly-fishing region in the United States and arguably one of the premiere fly-fishing areas in the world, the region around West Yellowstone attracted thousands of fly-fishers every year.

Departing Massachusetts after transferring savings accounts, taking a distribution from a 401(k), and purchasing a silver Toyota

Tacoma pickup truck, he had turned away from his career in higher education and focused his future on his lifelong hobby of fly-fishing and his academic interest in geology. Surrounding himself with fly-fishing by living in West Yellowstone, where he also could engage in serious geological examinations and analyses, gave him the best of both worlds. No other place in the United States offered the combination of thermal and geological wonders intertwined with world-renowned fly-fishing. Three weeks after leaving Sturbridge, with what was left of his personal belongings under a tarpaulin stretched across the bed of the pickup, he was leasing a cabin on Duck Creek, eight miles north of West Yellowstone.

"Jim, have you had breakfast yet?" Parker asked. "I'm headed over to the Silver Spur, and if you want to join me, we could call Dick and meet him."

"I think Dick might already be there," responded Jim. "We can lock the shop for a little while until I get back. I don't expect much traffic for a while yet."

They locked the shop and walked across Canyon Street. Entering the Silver Spur Café, Parker saw Dick in a corner booth. "Morning, Dick. Have you ordered yet?"

"No, I haven't," responded Dick. "I was going through a list of fly-tying materials I need to order. I understand we have a fishing outing booked for Saturday morning with a friend of yours."

"Yes, so Jim tells me," replied Parker, "but this guy isn't what I would call a friend of mine. Jim, you need to clue us in about tomorrow and what you have set up. Let's order breakfast first, and then you can tell us what this fishing outing is all about."

Probably the most important decision Parker had made since plunging into the fly-shop business was the hiring of the two employees with whom he was now having breakfast. He had first hired Dick Wells, a longtime resident of the Yellowstone area who was an acclaimed expert fly-tier and knew more about fishing sites, conditions, insect hatches, and the when, where, and how of fishing in the Yellowstone region than Parker could hope to learn over the next several years. Dick had explained his interest in using his expertise to oversee and manage a fly shop without using his own resources. With Dick in charge of the shop, Parker knew he didn't have to be at the shop every day, all day.

The second employee hired was Jim Hill, a Colorado-born-and-bred young entrepreneur and a graduate of the University of Colorado Business School, where he had been a top student in his MBA class. Jim had been on the fast track to a high six-figure salary as an executive with REI when he left it all to become a fly-fishing and ski bum. After a year devoted to fishing and skiing, his severance pay and savings were gone, and he was in need of a job. With his business and organizational skills, he managed the business side of the shop—accounting, payables, catalog sales, Web sales, and inventory.

Reaching into his shirt pocket, Jim pulled out a sheet of paper. "Here's the list of names of the people your friend said would be joining him on Saturday."

Looking the list over, Parker said, "I know the names of two of these men, although I've never met them. Peter Garfield is the president of Allentown State University in Pennsylvania. The other name I recognize is Brian Carlson, president of Rosemont University in Illinois. I don't know the other guy or the two women. I wonder if they too are presidents of colleges or universities."

"They probably are, at least that's the impression I got from talking with your friend," responded Jim. "He said he was attending a meeting of university presidents at the Cutthroat Conference Center at Big Sky, so I'm assuming the other three people are also university presidents."

"So, what have you figured out about the fishing outing?" asked Parker.

"I thought we could reserve an eight-passenger van, which we'll use to transport the clients plus you and Dick to the Firehole River and then back again," responded Jim. "The clients could be dropped off two by two at three different spots along the river, and then, throughout the morning, the two of you could cruise back and forth and check how they are doing. I'll stay at the shop and around noon pick up some box lunches and drinks and meet all of you at the Fountain Flats picnic area for lunch."

"Sounds workable to me," responded Parker. "How about after lunch you and I trade places? I'll go back to the shop while you and Dick do the cruising. You should plan to pick up everyone around 4 and get back to the shop by 4:30 or so. That should leave plenty of time for the presidents to return to the conference center for whatever might be happening at their meeting."

They finished breakfast and were getting ready to leave when Parker's cell phone rang. The readout said the call was from the Cutthroat Conference Center. "Hello, Parker Williams speaking."

"Parker, Edgar Hickson here. Long time no see or talk with you. I still can't believe you gave up your position at Sturbridge for a fly shop out here in the boondocks. Listen, I want everything to go like clockwork on Saturday. I expect to catch lots of fish, have good food and drink, and get back to this place by 6. A lot of people want to meet me, especially once they learn I'm up for the President of the Year Award."

"Edgar, don't worry," responded Parker, "everything has been planned, and we will be set to go when you get here. Relax and enjoy yourself at the meeting. I'll see you tomorrow morning, and we can catch up then."

"I sure hope you know what you're talking about," replied Edgar. "You're being paid big bucks for this outing, so I expect to be treated appropriately. And one other thing, Peter Garfield has also been nominated for the President of the Year Award, so I want you to make sure he and I fish together. I'm going to persuade him to withdraw his name before he is embarrassed when I walk away with the award. He doesn't have a prayer. Actually, nobody would, up against me. I'm the obvious choice since I'm the only president worthy of the award. He needs to understand that and bow out."

Chapter Two
May 23
Saturday

Following a night of restlessness and little sleep, Parker found himself driving to the fly shop in the dark. He wasn't sure how much he had slept, but it certainly wasn't more than a few hours. His mind kept going over aspects of the upcoming day, checking off the numerous details to make sure they had been completed and nothing was being overlooked.

The first light of dawn was spreading across the sky as he turned the key to unlock the fly shop. Flicking on the lights, he felt a wave of satisfaction wash over him as he surveyed the organized interior. On the east wall were the Sage fly rods, glistening in their wall display. A large case of flies—dries, nymphs, soft hackels, and streamers— dominated the middle of the shop. Along the west and south walls were numerous racks of fly-tying materials for those fly-fishers who wanted quality materials for the flies they tied. Throughout the rest of the shop were displays of waders, float tubes, shirts, hats, and the numerous gadgets of all shapes and sizes that were so popular with the weekend fly-fishers.

Looking up, he saw a large white van pull up and park in front of the fly shop. Dick jumped out of the driver's side and entered the shop. "Looks like Jim did a good job in selecting a van big enough to hold everyone," said Parker.

"Yeah, it actually is assigned to the Bozeman area, but Missy at Big Sky Car Rental was able to get it for us," responded Dick. "Take a look at this." He showed Parker a Royal Wulff fly, which was one of a set of six he had in a small, grey fly box. "I tied these last night, and I plan to give one to each president as a gift from the Gold Medal Fly Shop."

"Another work of art," replied Parker as he examined the fly. "I almost hate to see it used; it's so exquisitely tied. Are the others as delicately tied as this one?"

"I hope so," responded Dick. "We can give the flies to them at lunch so they can use them in the afternoon in case fishing tails off and we need to jump-start their ability to catch fish during the afternoon."

Hearing the shop door open, Parker turned to see Laurie Black enter. Dressed in jeans and a misty-blue pullover with her hair pulled back in a pony tail, she had that youthful natural beauty that didn't require makeup. "Laurie, thanks again for helping out this weekend," said Parker. "As I said last night, Jim will be with you this morning, and I'll trade with him this afternoon. You will be on your own over lunch. Any problems with that?"

"None that I can think of," she responded. "I suspect most people coming in today will want permits to fish in the park and ask about which flies to use. There shouldn't be anything I can't handle as long as I don't get overwhelmed by too many people."

Laurie Black was a graduate student at Montana State University in Bozeman, where she was doing research on whirling disease for her master's degree thesis. For the past few years, she had worked part-time and summers in a sporting goods store while she was an undergraduate student at the University of Montana in Mizzoula. Consequently, she knew the ropes around a retail business, was comfortable with customers, could handle the cash register and credit card sales, and was sort of a Jill-of-all-trades around the fly shop.

As Parker was contemplating how the day with the presidents might unfold, two Ford Explorers pulled up in front of the fly shop. A man who Parker recognized as Edgar Hickson got out of the passenger's side of one, walked to the front door, and entered the shop. "If my eyes didn't tell me it was so, I wouldn't believe it," he said. "Parker Williams, you are a sight for sore eyes. I can't believe you live in such a god-forsaken corner of the world. Do you know that there aren't any sushi bars or wine discos for hundreds of miles? What do you do around here for fun?"

"Edgar, good to see you," responded Parker as they shook hands. "I bet you and the other presidents are eager to begin fishing. Let's get everyone acquainted, and I will explain the schedule to you. Then, we will take you to some wonderful fishing spots on the Firehole River."

Edgar looked like a walking advertisement for Orvis. He had so many gadgets hanging from his fishing vest that Parker wondered if he knew what even half of them were supposed to do. They all walked out of the shop to where the other presidents were standing. "Okay, let me introduce everyone," said Edgar. "Helen Whitmore, meet Parker Williams. As I told you during the ride, Parker was formerly president of Sturbridge State before something went loose in his head and he bailed out to come to this place."

Parker didn't know Helen Whitmore so he exchanged a handshake and a brief "nice to meet you" before Edgar introduced the other woman. "This is Sheila Morgan." Again, Parker shook hands and offered a welcome.

He then reached across to shake the hand of one of the men. "My name is Peter Garfield. I don't think we've ever met, but I did know about your being at Sturbridge. Nice to meet you."

Shaking his hand, Parker replied, "Nice to meet you too, Peter, and congratulations. Edgar told me you and he are both nominees for the President of the Year Award."

"Yes, it really was a surprise, the nomination I mean," responded Peter. "I know that Edgar thinks he is the only president qualified for the award, but I may just surprise him. You know, Edgar has alienated many people over the years, and I'm counting on that helping me."

Parker reached to shake the hand now extended to him. "I'm Brian Carlson. I don't think our paths ever crossed, but I was aware you were at Sturbridge. Edgar told us about your leaving Sturbridge and moving here. Quite a change, I'd say. When did you decide to open a fly shop?"

"Just a few months ago," responded Parker. "So far so good, but we are just beginning to get into the busy time for us, so we will see how it goes." Turning to the group, he said, "Let me introduce all of you to Dick Wells and Jim Hill. Both work with me, and they will be helping you today with your fishing. They are expert guides who know every inch of the Firehole River. If you will listen to them, you will catch fish."

"I'm sorry; I was getting my fly line on my rod." Stepping around from the back of one of the Explorers was a man wearing Simms chest waders and a Cortland fishing vest. "I'm Fred Wasson, and you must be Parker Williams. Edgar told us about you. Good to meet you." Parker noticed Wasson was casting his eyes nervously from side to side as if he were anticipating being caught off guard at any moment.

After making sure that each person's equipment was working properly and each had completed a fishing permit for Yellowstone National Park, they departed in the van with Dick driving and Parker riding shotgun. They drove fifteen miles along the Madison River to Madison Junction, where they turned right to follow the Firehole River. The two women were dropped first at Fountain Flats after Dick told them to fish elk hair caddis against the banks of the river. Fred Wasson and Brian Carlson were dropped at Ojo Caliente Spring while Peter Garfield and Edgar were dropped at Biscuit Basin. Dick and Parker spent the remainder of the morning driving from person to person, helping them read the water, spot rising trout, and replenish flies. Elk hair caddis were definitely working well. Parker was relieved that trout were being caught and released by everyone. The best advertisement for a guide service was clients catching fish and enjoying themselves.

Toward noon, Dick and Parker picked up the presidents and drove to the parking lot of the Fountain Flats picnic area where Jim had placed three picnic tables together. Gathering around the tables, Dick handed each president a box lunch and told them to choose a bottle of water or a can of juice or soda, which had been placed in a cooler earlier in the morning.

"I expected beer, not a kiddie's drink," said Edgar. "Can't someone make a run back to town and get us some Coors?"

"Sorry, Edgar, there is an understanding between the park and the fly-shop owners that neither beer nor other types of alcohol will be brought into the park when we bring clients to fish," responded Parker.

"What a stupid arrangement," said Edgar, "but what can you expect from people who live and work out here in the boondocks and have no class or culture."

"I'm going to trade places with Jim," Parker said to the presidents. "After we finish lunch here, Jim and Dick will take you back to some other fishing spots where the action should be as good as it was this morning."

"Wait a minute," said Edgar. "I want to make sure I get back to the conference center on time. Who's going to pick me up and when and where?"

"Don't be concerned, Edgar," responded Parker. "Jim and Dick will pick you up at predetermined places they will show you when they drop you off. Make sure you're at those spots by 4, and you won't have any trouble getting to the conference center on time."

"Before we head back to the river, I have a gift for each of you," said Dick. He was holding the small grey fly box containing the Royal Wulff flies he had shown Parker. "We want you to use these flies when you start fishing this afternoon." Dick gave each president a fly for which they all expressed thanks except Edgar.

"Let's get going," said Edgar. "There are trout just waiting for me to lay my fly in front of their noses."

After telling them he would see them in a few hours back at the fly shop, Parker took Jim's Jeep and headed back to West Yellowstone, where he spent the remainder of the afternoon waiting on customers and answering questions related to how fishing was in the park. People began to come back from their day's fishing and were gathering on the sidewalk in front of the shop to tell their stories and talk about the big one that got away. As the business in the shop began to decline, Parker's cell phone rang. The readout said the call was from Jim.

"Hi, Jim. What's going on?" asked Parker. "You about ready to head in?"

"I would if I could locate Edgar Hickson," responded Jim. "The other five presidents were all by the road at the assigned pickup spots, but not him."

Parker thought it odd that Edgar wasn't pacing the road at the prearranged place and time. He was the one who insisted on being back to the conference center on time. "I don't have a clue where he might be," responded Parker. "Are you sure you went to the prearranged place?"

"Yeah, and he wasn't there," responded Jim. "I waited for several minutes. I even walked down to the river to see if I could spot him. Then I drove back and forth along the road trying to locate him. The other presidents are saying that they need to get back to the conference center. What should I do?"

"We can't afford to have the other presidents ticked off with us because of Edgar," responded Parker. "Come on back to the shop. I'll figure out what to do about Edgar."

Parker wondered what Edgar was up to now. Was he purposefully making himself scarce? If so, why? Maybe Edgar wanted an excuse to be late so he could make a grand entrance at the conference center when he knew everyone would be present. Parker decided to wait for Jim to arrive with the five presidents and provide whatever assistance he could to finish their experience as a positive one. They would be anxious to get on their way to the conference center, and once they were gone, he would drive back along the Firehole River road, locate Edgar, and drive him directly to the conference center. There was still time to find Edgar and get him to the conference center by 6.

****

Thoughts flooded his mind during the fifteen-mile drive from West Yellowstone to Madison Junction. Calling park headquarters and alerting someone to what he was doing crossed his mind, but since Edgar wasn't a missing person, at least not yet, and Parker didn't know if he had injuries requiring on-site medical attention, calling would be premature. He decided he would first look for Edgar, and if he didn't find him or if he did find him and he was injured, he would then call park headquarters. Besides, Edgar was probably right now standing by the road fuming and cursing everyone and everything.

Parking the pickup next to the bridge by Ojo Caliente Spring, he walked down to the riverbank and looked up and down the river hoping to spot Edgar. The only thing he saw was an osprey cruising over the river hoping to spot a fish for supper, and the only sound he heard was that of the flow of the river. He thought that Edgar, being an inexperienced fisherman and also lazy, would wade downstream with the current rather than upstream against the current. Edgar probably didn't know that wading downstream could easily disturb fish and send them scattering for cover since they always faced upstream and could see or hear a person approaching.

Heading downstream and walking along the bank, he kept a watchful eye for any signs of a fisherman as well as muskrat holes. All he needed was a sprained or broken ankle or leg. He kept walking, wondering if he had misjudged the direction Edgar had waded. If Edgar did wade upstream, every step Parker took was making the distance greater between himself and where Edgar might be. He thought about turning around and decided he would after he got to the other side of the forested area he had entered. Before turning around, he wanted to be able to look quite a distance downstream from the clearing on the opposite end.

16

He walked slowly through the lodgepole pines, which were thick and hadn't been naturally pruned since the great fire of 1988. Most of the trees, which sprouted after the fire, were now eight to nine feet in height. They were so thick that from an airplane it looked like a green carpet had been spread across much of the park. Stepping around a particularly dense growth of young lodgepole pines, he saw that some were bent sideways at an angle from each other, like something large and heavy had forced them apart. Approaching the cluster of pines, he saw the outline of a dark object. Guessing it to be an elk or buffalo resting, he approached cautiously. Looking more closely, he saw that it wasn't an elk or buffalo, but a person, lying on its stomach. Waders, fishing vest, gadgets of all types hanging from the vest, and a net all confirmed what he dreaded to think—Edgar. He knelt down and looked closely. It was Edgar, no doubt about it. Edgar's face was to one side, and Parker could see that his eyes were open. Placing his ear next to Edgar's partially opened mouth, he heard no breathing. Placing his finders on Edgar's neck, he felt no pulse. Edgar was dead.

ROYAL WULFF

Hook: "Dry fly"

Tail: Dark elk hair

Body: Peacock herl butt then red floss followed by peacock
             herl tuff

Wing: White calf tail divided

Hackle: Brown saddle

Thread: 6/0 black monochord

1. Tie in dark brown elk hair for tail.
2. Tie in white calf tail, leaving long fibers. Tie into wing and divide wing in half.Tie under front and back to separate wings.
3. Wrap thread back to tail and attach two peacock herl strands.
4. Wrap peacock herl forward and tie in red floss.
5. Wrap floss forward and tie off.
6. Tie in two dark brown saddle hackles. Wrap hackle forward with equal wraps behind and in front of the wing.

ELK HAIR CADDIS

Hook:	"Dry fly"
Body:	Hare's ear dubbing in olive, brown, or grey
Ribbing:	.005" diameter gold wire
Wing:	Cream Colorado elk flank hair; some lighter, some darker
Hackle:	Dark brown grizzly palmered
Thread:	6/0 olive, brown, or gray to match body color

1. Tie in a 4" piece of gold wire at the bend of the hook. Apply some dubbing to the thread.
2. Dub a body forward.
3. Tie in hackle at the eye of the hook, allowing 1/5 of the shank to tie in the wing.
4. Push the hackle backwards and tie down.
5. Wind gold wire up through hackle and tie off at eye.
6. Even a small bunch of light elk hair. Holding the wing between thumb and forefinger, tie in the wing with several loose wraps. Then make several tight wraps to hold wing in place and flair the hair.
7. Even off fibers. Trim over the head.
8. Whip finish and lacquer.

Chapter Three

Parker knew enough from watching television crime shows and from his former experiences with campus police forces at the universities where he had worked that he shouldn't do anything to the body or the area around it. He hadn't seen any signs of a struggle, and as he looked more carefully, he still didn't. Carefully bending down to look closely at the ground immediately next to the body, he didn't see any sign of blood. He surmised that Edgar might have gone into the trees to relieve himself and succumbed to an abrupt heart attack. Looking more closely at Edgar's face, it appeared to be bloated. Maybe Edgar had stumbled while wading and swallowed some water, which caused him to panic, which, in turn, had triggered a heart attack.

Knowing he had to call someone at park headquarters to report finding Edgar's body, he punched in the number for park headquarters and asked for the Security Office. A man, identifying himself as the director of security, answered. "Bruce Perkins speaking. How may I be of assistance?"

"Mr. Perkins, my name is Parker Williams. I've just discovered a body near Ojo Caliente Spring on the bank of the Firehole River. I'm calling to inform you and ask what I should do."

"You said you're by Ojo Caliente Spring?" responded Perkins. "Are you sure the person is dead?"

"Yes, I'm sure he is dead," responded Parker. "I checked his pulse and listened for any breathing. I'm about one-half mile downstream of the spring in a stand of lodgepole pines along the riverbank."

"Okay, Mr. Williams," said Perkins, "don't do anything to disturb the body or the area around it. I'll come myself and also have an ambulance sent. Can you leave the body for a few minutes and walk out to the road so we know where you are?"

"Sure," responded Parker. "Nothing is going to happen to the body if I leave it. I'll wait about fifteen minutes and then walk out to the road and signal you."

He walked to the road, and after only a few minutes, he saw a Chevy Tahoe of the National Park Service and an ambulance approaching. Funny, he thought, an ambulance had to be dispatched even though it wouldn't be needed. Regulations and cover your rear end in case of liability, he guessed as the reasons for the ambulance. Like any bureaucracy, the lawyers had convinced everyone that regulations were to be followed, regardless of how foolish it might be to do so.

He signaled, and the Tahoe pulled over. A man and a woman, both dressed in the national park official green uniforms, exited. "I take it you're Mr. Williams. I'm Bruce Perkins, the director of security. We talked on the phone. This is Jessica Samuels, my assistant. If you would, please take us to the body."

The two ambulance attendants joined them, one carrying a stretcher and the other a medical satchel and a body bag. Parker stood back while the two ambulance attendants checked Edgar for vital signs. Finding none, they cautiously turned his body over. There wasn't any blood visible on Edgar's face or neck. Since he was wearing chest waders, Parker couldn't see his chest area, but his fishing vest didn't appear disturbed.

While the ambulance attendants were checking the body more carefully, Bruce and Jessica secured the area with yellow tape. When the attendants had finished, Bruce took pictures of the body, as well as the area surrounding the body, while Jessica took samples of the bark of the trees that had been bent by the weight of the body. Bruce reached into Edgar's fishing-vest pocket and withdrew a Yellowstone National Park fishing permit. It was the one that Parker helped Edgar fill out at the shop. The name Edgar Hickson was printed in the space for the name. Bruce asked Parker if he could identify the body. "Yes, this is Edgar Hickson, no doubt in my mind," said Parker. The two attendants then placed the body into the body bag and carried it to the ambulance. In the meantime, Bruce and Jessica were on all fours examining the ground where the body had been resting. Both had tweezers, and although the sun was shining, they used small flashlights with an intense beam to examine the ground. Parker saw Jessica place a few small items into plastic bags, which she labeled with the location where she had found the item. He was too far away to determine what the items were.

"There doesn't appear to be any foul play involved nor are there any signs of a struggle or the presence of an animal," said Bruce. "I'd speculate this man drowned since he seems to have swallowed a good deal of water. He may have had a heart attack, fell into the water, swallowed a great deal of it, stumbled here into the trees, and then died from an inability to breathe. But nothing is for certain until an autopsy is performed. That will take a few days since the body will have to be taken to the coroner's office in Jackson."

"What about notification of next of kin?" asked Parker. "I think he was divorced, and I don't know about children."

"My office will take care of proper notification," responded Bruce. "We will do that back at headquarters. We will also have to determine to whom the body will eventually be released. Any help you can give us with names of family or relatives would be appreciated."

"I suggest you contact the university where he is president," responded Parker. "Someone there should be able to provide you with the information you need about family or relatives."

"I'm planning to contact the Billings Office of the FBI and let them know what happened," said Bruce. "I need to point out to them the possibility that this might be a homicide. If the autopsy results do show the cause of death as foul play, we will want to request the assistance of the FBI. A homicide investigation isn't something that we are equipped to handle by ourselves."

Bruce told Parker that he would like to have a statement from him. He said he would again be contacting Parker to verify his statement and give him an opportunity to add any details that he might fail to remember now. Parker described the day's events. Bruce didn't ask any questions, but allowed Parker to talk uninterrupted. When he finished, Bruce asked him for the names of all the other people that had contact with Edgar during the day. He also asked how each could be contacted. Parker added that he didn't know how long the presidents' meeting was scheduled to last, so Bruce might want to focus first on contacting the five other presidents at the Yellowstone Conference Center.

"Mr. Williams, please don't leave West Yellowstone until you hear from me," said Bruce. "Where is your car parked?"

"I parked my pickup by the bridge at Ojo Caliente Spring and walked down the riverbank to here," responded Parker. "Why do you ask?"

"I want to examine your pickup before you leave," responded Bruce.

"Wait a minute, you don't think I had anything to do with Edgar's death, do you?" asked Parker. "I wasn't anywhere near him all afternoon. I only came looking for him after he didn't show up when he was supposed to be picked up."

"Mr. Williams, I'm not accusing you of anything, but until we know how and when this guy died, I have to include everyone as possibly being involved in his death," responded Bruce. "Standard procedure for these types of things, I'm sure you understand. Now, if you'll take me to your pickup, Jessica will pick me up after I'm finished examining it."

****

Driving back to West Yellowstone, he kept playing the scene over and over again in his mind. Edgar's body in the trees, the appearance of no foul play, Edgar decked out in the finest fishing clothes and accessories, Bruce and Jessica picking up small objects and placing them in plastic bags, and Bruce considering Parker a suspect should the autopsy reveal that foul play was involved in Edgar's death. He suddenly sat upright, which caused him to almost lose control of the pickup. Edgar's fly rod. He hadn't seen it by Edgar's body, nor did he recall seeing it on the bank of the river. Granted, he hadn't been looking specifically for the fly rod. He had been too shocked from discovering Edgar's body to think much about anything else, especially when Bruce Perkins said he needed to examine his pickup. It was only now that he thought about Edgar's fly rod. Neither Bruce nor Jessica had mentioned it, so they too must have overlooked it. Perhaps the fly rod was lying in the trees, having been thrown there by Edgar when he felt a heart attack coming on more strongly. Another possibility was that Edgar had first felt a heart attack while standing in the river fishing and had struggled before falling in the river and, in doing so, dropped the fly rod into the river. If this is what happened, it would have floated until it either became lodged against a submerged tree or set of boulders, or continued to float, being swept into the Firehole River Canyon. If that happened, the rough water flowing over the boulders and rocks of the canyon probably smashed the fly rod into pieces.

Thinking he should alert Bruce Perkins to the missing fly rod, he pulled out his cell phone to call him but then realized Bruce probably wouldn't be back to his office yet. He would only be leaving a voice-mail message. Instead, he called the fly shop. Dick answered. "Dick, I have some bad news. Edgar Hickson is dead. I found his body among some pine trees on the bank of the river downstream from Ojo Caliente Spring. The Security Office of the park has done a preliminary investigation."

"I can't believe it," said Dick. "How did he die?"

"Can't be sure, but my guess is that he had a heart attack," answered Parker. "There didn't appear to be any foul play, no blood or signs of a struggle. The actual cause of death won't be known until after an autopsy is performed. That will take a few days, especially since this is Memorial Day weekend."

"This doesn't seem real," said Dick. "I just saw Edgar a few hours ago, and now he is dead."

"Tell you what I would like for you to do," said Parker. "Contact as many of the guides as you can and ask them to come to an early morning meeting at the Timberline Café. Tell them I will buy breakfast. That should help get them there. I will contact Jim and Laurie and ask them to also attend. And, Dick, let's keep the news of Edgar's death to ourselves for now."

Entering his cabin, he saw the message light on the telephone flashing. Punching the replay button, he heard Bruce Perkins' voice. "Mr. Williams, call me first thing in the morning."

Chapter Four
Sunday
May 24

Parking in front of the Timberline Café a few minutes before 6:30, Parker recognized several of the pickups, Jeeps, and old Suburbans also parked along the front of the café, indicating that Dick, Jim, and most, if not all, of the guides were already inside. Entering the café, the smell of bacon permeated the air. How he enjoyed that smell. Bacon was something he knew he shouldn't eat because of the high fat content, but yet, he couldn't ever say no to it whenever it was in his presence.

Dick and the guides were seated in the large corner booth. Parker had been able to contact Jim last night, but he had been unable to reach Laurie. They were now both seated at a table adjacent to the booth. When he called Jim last night, he thought he heard a woman's voice in the background. Since Laurie wasn't at her mother's home when Parker tried to reach her, he wondered if Laurie had spent the night with Jim. Looking at them now, he couldn't tell.

"Thanks for coming in this early," he said as he slipped into the booth next to Dick. "Before I get to why I wanted to meet all of you this morning, I want to thank you for your work of the past few days. We seem to be off to a good start, and it all comes down to the quality service you are providing our customers."

He could sense that while they appreciated being patted on the back, they all wanted him to get to the point of the meeting. They were apprehensive since they didn't know why they had been summoned. "I wanted all of you to be in the same place when I told you some disturbing news. Yesterday, we hosted a fishing outing for six clients, actually they were all university presidents. Dick and Jim did a fantastic job of organizing the outing and covering all the details. When Jim went to pick up the clients, only five were at their assigned pickup places. The sixth person wasn't at his. Jim and I decided not to have the other five clients wait while we searched for him, so Jim drove them in to the shop, and they then went back to their meeting at the Cutthroat Conference Center. I went back to Ojo Caliente Spring to see if I could find our missing client. I did find him about a half-mile downstream from the spring. When I found him, he was dead."

Laurie gasped, and several of the guides mumbled under their breath. Jim reached across the table and took Laurie's hand, looking incredulously at Parker. "Was he dead when you found him?" asked Dave, the crusty guide from Island Park, Idaho, who usually guided customers on the Henry's Fork River. "What did he die from?"

"He was dead when I found him," responded Parker. "How he died, I don't know, and we won't know for sure until an autopsy is completed. It looked to me like he died from natural causes, probably a heart attack is my guess. But until the results of an autopsy are known, it is anyone's guess."

"What do you think happened?" asked Jim.

"My guess is that he managed to struggle to shore, where he collapsed on the bank and died in the trees," responded Parker. "But, again, we won't know for sure until an autopsy is performed. Until then, park officials are handling it like a possible homicide, which means they will want to talk with everyone who had contact with Edgar yesterday."

"If he had a heart attack, why are they thinking it may be a homicide?" asked Dave.

"Dave, I didn't say for sure he had a heart attack," responded Parker. "I'm guessing that it was a heart attack since I didn't see any signs of foul play nor did the park officials who examined the body and the area around it. But until it is verified by an autopsy that he died from a natural cause, park regulations dictate that it be handled as if it were a homicide."

"Will this affect our business?" asked Paul, a guide specializing in wading trips on the Madison River in the Cliff-Wade area of the river. "I've got bills to pay and can't afford to lose my income."

"I hope it doesn't hurt our business, Paul, but we really can't control that," responded Parker. "All we can do is cooperate with the authorities and continue to provide the best service to our customers we are capable of giving. We are fortunate this is a holiday weekend, so news like this will most likely get lost in the hustle and bustle of the weekend. But, we must be prepared to deal with whatever comes."

"Do you think some of us will be interviewed by the park's security people?" asked Dick.

"You, Laurie, and Jim should expect to be contacted by Bruce Perkins of the park's Security Office," said Parker. "He will want a statement from each of you about how and when you were in contact with Edgar. He may try to contact you today, although Sunday isn't usually a day that park officials work, but a death in the park isn't normal business, so he may be anxious to contact you as soon as he can."

Parker's cell phone rang. The readout said the call was from the Security Office of Yellowstone National Park. He remembered that Bruce Perkins had left a voice-mail message. Glancing at his watch, it was still early, so it was obvious Bruce was anxious to reach him. "Hello, this is Parker Williams speaking."

"Mr. Williams, Bruce Perkins here. Jessica and I are on our way to the Cutthroat Conference Center to interview each of the five presidents, and I want to verify their names again with you. I have Peter Garfield, Brian Carlson, Fred Wasson, Helen Whitmore, and Sheila Morgan. Are these the names of the presidents on the fishing trip?"

"Yes, those are the right names," responded Parker.

Bruce continued. "I also contacted the head of the public relations office at Northern Missouri University to inform them of Hickson's death. The woman I talked with was able to give me the name of a daughter, so I contacted her before calling you this morning. She lives in Virginia. After the autopsy, she said she would come to Bozeman to claim the body and would be accompanying it back to Virginia. I also had voice-mail messages, one from the Northern Missouri University campus newspaper and the other from the *Morning Star Gazette*, the local community newspaper. I provided no details other than to verify that Hickson had died while fly-fishing in Yellowstone National Park. I want you to know that I didn't mention that he was part of a fishing outing hosted by the Gold Medal Fly Shop. I figured that you didn't need that type of publicity."

"Thanks for being sensitive to the potential public relations impact on my business," said Parker. "I didn't know Edgar had a daughter. You probably should expect to be contacted by some, if not all, of the media in the community. By the way, Bruce, did you happen to pick up Edgar's fly rod?"

"His fly rod? Now that you mention it, I didn't see his fly rod," responded Bruce.

"My guess is if he had a heart attack, he probably dropped it into the river when he felt his heart attack coming on," said Parker. "By now, it is probably in a dozen pieces somewhere in the Firehole River Canyon."

"Mr. Williams, remember that until the autopsy is complete and we have the results, I am treating this as a homicide," said Bruce. "There is no assurance that Edgar died from a heart attack."

"Bruce, you can't be serious about Edgar being murdered," said Parker. "He was out in the river by himself. You saw the body. There were no signs of any foul play, no blood." In saying this, Parker realized that with no witnesses and no apparent foul play, if Edgar had been murdered, it could be a perfect crime.

"I am serious, very serious," responded Bruce. "Until I hear something different, I'm treating this as a homicide. Please let your employees know that I intend to contact them today to arrange for their statements. And, don't forget, until a homicide is ruled out, you are a suspect along with them."

Saying goodbye, Parker realized his side of the conversation with Bruce had been overheard by Dick, Jim, Laurie, and the guides. They were looking at him with a combination of curiosity and apprehension, anticipating that he would fill them in on Bruce's part of the conversation.

"That was Bruce Perkins, the director of security for the park," said Parker. "He said he was going to interview the five presidents that were part of the fishing outing yesterday. He wanted to verify he had the correct names and to tell me that he had contacted Northern Missouri University and informed them of Edgar's death. Edgar's daughter in Virginia will be coming to claim the body after the autopsy. Since Edgar's death is being considered a homicide until ruled out by an autopsy, any of you that had contact with Edgar yesterday will be contacted sometime today by Bruce to arrange an interview with either him or his assistant."

As the meeting broke up, Parker asked Dick, Jim, and Laurie to stay. The guides had individual clients they were meeting at the shop whom they would go with either to fish from a float boat on the Madison River below Quake Lake or to fish by wading the Madison, Firehole, or Gibbon rivers in the park.

"Are each of you planning to work in the shop today?" asked Parker. They all answered they were. "Okay, then, you can probably give your statements today to Bruce or his assistant using the backroom of the shop. I would like to take a few hours now to look into a certain matter, so if it's okay with you, I'll be gone for a few hours."

"Sure," "No problem," "Fine with me," they responded in turn. They said they didn't have plans for the day and intended to be in the fly shop.

****

Feeling uncertain as he headed toward Madison Junction and from there along the Firehole River, Parker convinced himself of his intention to look for Edgar's fly rod. He knew that if Edgar had a heart attack while fishing, he certainly would have dropped his fly rod as he struggled toward the riverbank and eventually into the trees. At least, that is how Parker pictured the scene surrounding Edgar's death. If this was the way it happened, then his initial assumption that the fly rod floated down the river until it lodged against a submerged tree or some boulders was probably true. Although the possibility remained that it floated all the way to the Firehole River Canyon and was dashed to pieces, this seemed to be a long shot since the canyon was nearly seven miles from where Edgar had been fishing. There were numerous places before the canyon where a nine-foot fly rod could get tangled in trees or weed beds, or wedged between some boulders.

The No Parking/No Stopping signs still lined the shoulder of the road directly adjacent to the area where Parker had discovered Edgar's body. Yellow tape and orange cones also remained in place, and a Yellowstone National Park Chevy Tahoe was parked along the road, but no park security staff or rangers were visible. Knowing that the yellow tape and orange cones served to draw curious passersby like honey draws flies, he anticipated a traffic jam occurring later in the morning if the tape and cones remained.

Parking his pickup downroad from the signs, he pulled his waders from behind his seat and slipped them on. He walked down to the bank of the river and waded into the river a few yards downstream from the area now cordoned off by the tape. He headed downstream, reading the water much like he would do if he were fishing, only now he wasn't looking for where trout might be lurking. Instead, he was looking for places where the current flowed between boulders or through overgrowth or over submerged trees, any place where the flow of the river suggested that a nine-foot fly rod could become wedged or hung up.

It was slow going. He had to wade from one side of the river to the other. By focusing on an object on the opposite bank, he made sure he didn't veer off his path and miss some spots. Various sizes of branches of lodgepole pines were wedged between and behind boulders or in jams of wood and debris, but no fly rod. His enthusiasm for the task waned as it became increasingly probable that if Edgar had dropped his fly rod into the water, it might now be in several pieces in the Firehole River Canyon.

Entertaining thoughts of quitting, a flash of reflected sunlight from something over where the current flowed into a tight wedge between two large boulders caught his eye. Wading over and looking more closely at the wedge of water, he saw bobbing in the strong current the tip of a fly rod, the gold ferule at the tip reflecting the sun. Reaching under the water, he grabbed the fly rod and pulled it out of the water. It was a Sage, the kind Edgar had been using. Examining the butt end of the fly rod and the fly reel, he noticed the initials E.H. were stamped on the fly rod just above the reel seat. E.H.—Edgar Hickson. Parker knew he had found Edgar's fly rod.

Chapter Five

Pulling out his cell phone, Parker called park headquarters and asked for Bruce Perkins in the Security Office. The receptionist responded that Mr. Perkins was at the Cutthroat Conference Center and could be reached via his cell phone. He must be interviewing the presidents, thought Parker. He punched in Bruce's cell phone number hoping he would answer.

"Hello, this is Bruce Perkins."

"Bruce, it's Parker Williams. Your receptionist gave me your cell phone number. I wanted to let you know I found Edgar's fly rod. Right now, I'm standing in the Firehole River holding it in my hand. Should I take it with me to my shop, leave it with whomever from the park that might be in this area, or do you want me to keep it and give it directly to you?"

"Wait a minute," responded Bruce. "Where did you say you found it and when?"

"I just found it," responded Parker. "It was wedged between some rocks in the river, not too far from where I found Edgar's body."

"Mr. Williams, you realize the fly rod could be material evidence, so be careful how you handle it. Be especially careful that you don't cover fingerprints." Bruce's voice became louder and more strident as he talked. "And, since when do you take it upon yourself to do your own investigative work? I told you that until we know how Edgar died, you weren't to do anything regarding this investigation. What don't you understand about what I said?"

"I couldn't get it out of my mind that Edgar's fly rod was missing," responded Parker. "I had some time this morning, so I thought I would look for it. As I said, I found it a little downstream from where I found Edgar's body. It was wedged between two boulders in the water. As far as I can tell, everything is intact, including the fly reel and fly line. I obviously have already handled the rod since I had to get it out of the water, but I've been careful; I haven't touched the handle."

"Make sure you don't," said Bruce. "Bring it to your shop. I will pick it up there. Again, be careful with it. Don't handle it any more than you have to and try not to handle it where there might be fingerprints."

"Bruce, have you heard anything about an autopsy?" asked Parker.

"No, not yet, but we are fortunate," responded Bruce. "The coroner is working today. We should have the results sometime this evening, or so he told me when I talked to him earlier today. Now, get away from that area and stop playing detective."

As Parker shifted the fly rod in his hand to avoid holding it on the handle, he noticed quite a bit of fly line was still out. Reeling it in, he paid special attention not to grasp the reel so that his fingers wouldn't overlap where Edgar's fingers most likely had rested. This made for slow going. Eventually, he saw the end of the fly line. Still attached were the leader, tippet, and even a fly. Looking carefully at the water-logged fly, he saw it was a Royal Wulff. Looking more closely and without touching it, he thought it was the same Royal Wulff fly Dick had tied and given Edgar. No mistaking the perfection that was Dick's trademark.

Wading across the river to the bank closest to the road, he held the fly rod by the middle section. It bowed on either end, giving the impression he was carrying an arc. Stepping out of the river and walking back to his pickup, he laid the fly rod in the rear of the cab, placing a small cloth over the reel and handle. As he started to peel off his waders, his cell phone rang. It was Beth Richardson.

Beth Richardson was the assistant superintendent of Yellowstone National Park. She was the most striking and attractive woman Parker had laid eyes on in a long time. Even in the drab green unisex uniform of the National Park Service, which wasn't the most flattering outfit a woman could wear, whenever she was in a room with men, Parker had noticed that every man ended up staring at her. She was a classic beauty. Her shimmering auburn hair cascaded to her shoulders in subtle waves. With an alabaster complexion, set off by warm sparkling blue eyes, full but not heavy lips, perfect white teeth, and a sculptured chin, she oozed femininity without frailty. Also, there was no questioning she was a woman, as she filled out the uniform in all the proper proportions without being too ample or lean anywhere.

Parker had known Beth for several months, beginning when they were both part of a geological evaluation team investigating the impact of earthquakes on the underground thermal activity in the Old Faithful Geyser Basin. Their mutual interest in the geological wonders of the park had brought them together several times, but always as part of a study or evaluation team.

"Parker, I heard from Bruce Perkins that you found a body by the Firehole River. I'm worried about you. Are you okay?"

"Yes, Beth, I'm fine," he said. "Thanks for asking. I'm sorry I didn't call you myself to tell you about finding Edgar's body, but I've been preoccupied with Edgar's death and with Bruce Perkins of your Security Office. In fact, I just found Edgar's fly rod wedged between some boulders in the Firehole River. I don't know if it is going to shed any more light on Edgar's death, but it bothered me that it was missing. So, I went to look for it. I'm afraid I may have made your friend Mr. Perkins angry."

"Oh, don't worry about Bruce," said Beth. "Our security people are all alike. They don't think anyone else is capable of doing security work. I'm sure he will get over it soon enough. I have something to ask you, and I'll understand if you say no, given what you're going through. There is a lecture tonight on whirling disease at the Old Faithful auditorium. I was wondering if you would care to join me?"

He was so taken aback by her invitation that he had trouble responding. He hoped she hadn't taken his silence as a sign of his disinterest. "Sounds great, Beth. I'd love to join you. Who's giving the lecture and what time should I meet you?"

"Dr. Stuart Kennington of the Whirling Disease Institute. Remember when we helped the Trout Unlimited group do the electroshocking of the Madison River and were surprised by how many rainbow trout had whirling disease? We had said then we wanted to learn more about the disease. This is a wonderful opportunity to hear about it from an expert. The lecture starts at 7:30."

"I'll be there on time," said Parker. "And thanks again for asking me."

Driving back to the shop, he kept going over in his mind the numerous tasks he knew awaited him at the shop. He needed to spend the remainder of the day catching up since there would be no time tomorrow given it was Memorial Day. A host of customers would be coming into the shop in the morning to check on fishing conditions and to purchase flies and various odds and ends for their fishing day. As he turned onto Canyon Street, he spotted Bryson Haggerty walking across the street to the Gray Wolf Pharmacy.

Bryson Haggerty had moved to West Yellowstone a couple of years before Parker. He was an avid fisherman and also was deeply involved in the wolf restoration program of the park. Parker hadn't thought much about it when he had first learned that Haggerty and Edgar Hickson once had been employed at the same university at the same time, but now he reflected back on what he had learned about the two. He remembered that Haggerty and Edgar went back several years, and for at least as long as Parker had known about Haggerty, he had been told that bad blood existed between Edgar and Haggerty. He wondered if Haggerty knew about Edgar's death. Probably not, since Haggerty was known as a loner and usually wasn't too communicative with anyone or involved in any community activities. Parker also remembered that Haggerty had stopped in the fly shop a few days ago and had said he was going to fish the Firehole River on Saturday. Parker wondered if Haggerty and Edgar had met each other yesterday and, if they had, if Haggerty had any information about Edgar—how he looked or how he was feeling. Parker decided to see if he could talk with Haggerty for a few minutes.

Haggerty was standing at the checkout counter when Parker entered the pharmacy. "Parker, good to see you," said Bob Storey, the owner of the pharmacy. Like Parker, Bob had opened the pharmacy only a few months earlier. A pharmacist who had moved to West Yellowstone two years earlier, Bob and his wife had come to West Yellowstone when he decided to retire. He had been a pharmacist for thirty-five years in various King Soopers and Safeway stores in the Denver, Colorado, area. Bob had told Parker that he had flunked retirement. It wasn't what he thought it would be, so he purchased a vacant store on Canyon Street and opened the Gray Wolf Pharmacy.

"Good to see you too, Bob," said Parker. "Hope business is good." Turning to Bryson Haggerty, he said, "Hello to you too, Bryson."

Haggerty nodded but made no attempt to acknowledge Parker. He looked only at Bob and asked what he owed. "Bryson, did you hear the sad news?" asked Parker. Again, no acknowledgment from Haggerty. "A mutual acquaintance of ours died yesterday. Edgar

Hickson. Quite unexpectedly. He was fishing the Firehole River. Did you happen to see him yesterday while you were fishing the Firehole?"

Haggerty turned to face Parker with a glare in his eyes that caused Parker to step back. "No, I didn't see him yesterday, and I'm not sorry to hear about his death," said Haggerty. "He was a mean-spirited person, and I hope his soul rots in hell."

Hurrying out of the store, Haggerty brushed past Parker. Parker turned to Bob Storey. "What do you make of that? He sure seemed to be in a hurry to get out of here once he saw me."

"Let me tell you, Parker, he was as nervous as a cockroach in a frying pan all the time he was here," responded Bob. "I asked him if I could help him find what he was looking for. He wanted to know if I stocked monkshood poison. I told him I didn't nor would any legitimate pharmacy. That stuff is a lethal poison. Kills quickly. I wanted to ask him why he wanted the stuff, but I kept my mouth shut. Then you entered the store, and he couldn't wait to get out of here. You and he have some trouble between ya?"

"Not that I know about," responded Parker.

He thanked Bob and walked out of the store toward the fly shop. As he was crossing Canyon Street, he heard someone calling his name. He turned to see Lieutenant Hal Gamby of the Gallatin County Sheriff's office on the other side of the street. "Parker, wait a minute," Gamby said.

Hal Gamby was someone to avoid as far as Parker was concerned, but there was no obvious way to walk away without him realizing that Parker was trying to avoid him. Gamby was a small fish in a little pond who wanted to be a big fish in a little pond. He liked to throw his weight around, and he had considerable weight to throw around. He didn't realize his reputation around town was that he was a token on the sheriff's force and that he held onto his job only because he was a shirttail relative of Montana's governor and thus the sheriff was unwilling to put him out to pasture.

"Parker, I heard about the death of one of your clients and that you found the body. Do you know the cause of death yet?" He asked this question in a condescending manner as if he knew the cause of death and wanted Parker to ask him what it was.

"Hal, how did you hear about the death?" asked Parker.

"Karen Black told me," responded Gamby.

Parker remembered that Karen Black had been helping Gamby with a real-estate deal. He guessed that Laurie had told her mother what Parker had told Laurie and the guides at breakfast, and Karen must have then told Gamby.

Karen Black was a divorcée who had moved from Los Angeles to West Yellowstone with her daughter, Laurie, about five years earlier. Having worked in a real-estate agency in L.A., she saw an opportunity in West Yellowstone to establish her own agency and capitalize on the growing interest in the West Yellowstone and Southwestern Montana area by young retirees and owners of second homes. Ted Turner, Robert Redford, and the movie *A River Runs Through It* had brought publicity and notoriety to the area, which had translated into growing interest in Big Sky Country as a place to live and recreate.

"Hal, I'd like to visit, but I need to get back to the shop," said Parker.

He quickly moved ahead toward the shop. Dick, Jim, and Laurie were waiting on customers when Parker entered. He put thoughts of Edgar, Edgar's fly rod, Bryson Haggerty, and Lt. Hal Gamby out of his mind, spending the remainder of the day catching up on paperwork and helping with odds and ends around the shop. At 5:00, he said, "See you tomorrow," and left to go to his cabin. He planned to shave, shower, grab something to eat, and drive to the Old Faithful amphitheater to meet Beth Richardson.

As he shaved and showered, he felt apprehension growing as he thought about the evening before him. Quit acting like a teenager, he told himself. You and Beth are adults, and tonight is only about friendship and some companionship. She obviously didn't want to attend the lecture alone. Why she asked him to accompany her, rather than the numerous men that would fall all over themselves to be with her, was what he couldn't figure out.

Driving to the Old Faithful area, he again thought about how much he disliked Hal Gamby. He hardly knew him, but his mannerisms and pompous attitude bugged Parker. Perhaps it was because in his own way, Hal Gamby reminded Parker of several university presidents, and Parker wanted to forget those aspects of his former life. He would just have to try to avoid Hal and when that proved impossible, spend as little time around him as possible.

Chapter Six

Parker pulled into parking lot B next to the Old Faithful amphitheater a few minutes before 7:30. He had dressed in khaki Dockers and a button-down, light-weight, French-blue chamois shirt. He had even used some shave cologne, something he hadn't remembered doing in quite some time. Funny, he thought, it isn't that Beth and I haven't been around each other before, but here I am concerned with how I'm dressed and smell, as if this was the first time I was going to be around her.

He could remember when the parking area for Old Faithful was one lot, and a rather small one at that. Several years earlier, the National Park Service had received a special appropriation from Congress to redo the parking area and the entry/exit roads to the Old Faithful geyser area. Now there were several large parking lots and a divided, two-lane entry/exit road. The story told around town was that an influential congressman from the Midwest was on a trip with his family to Yellowstone National Park, and when they tried to park to see Old Faithful, there was no spot in the small parking lot. Consequently, they missed the eruption of the world's most famous geyser. Of course, given the congressman's schedule, the family couldn't stay for the next eruption, even though it would have been approximately one hour later. Miffed that there was no parking spot, the congressman pushed through an appropriation the next year to provide funds for additional parking lots and the divided, two-lane entry/exit road.

Entering the foyer of the amphitheater, he spotted Beth waiting by the information kiosk that flanked the west entrance to the amphitheater. She hadn't seen him yet, and so he had an opportunity to study her, even if it was from a distance. Dressed in a casual jean skirt with a soft pale-pink blouse, she looked radiant. As he walked toward her, she saw him and waved. He took in her perfect complexion, white teeth, and auburn hair which she wore this evening in a French twist.

"Hi. Was the drive okay?" she asked. "You never know what you might run into this time of year given this is the beginning of the tourist season."

"The drive was fine," he responded. "No traffic tie-ups. And you look marvelous. Not that you don't at other times, but the casual Western look is quite becoming."

"Thank you," she said. "You don't look too bad yourself, even for an owner of a fly shop." Her eyes sparkled as she talked, and Parker detected a slight smile that conveyed her sense of humor.

As they entered the auditorium and took seats on the side aisle about halfway down, he spotted Bryson Haggerty sitting on the other side of the auditorium near the rear. He was tempted to go over to him and see if he could find out why he had been so evasive at the pharmacy. But he would have to excuse himself from Beth, and he didn't want her to think he had something more important to do than talk with her. Perhaps he could intercept Haggerty immediately after the lecture and talk to him then.

The lecture was just the proper length with the right mix of slides showing the effects of whirling disease on juvenile rainbow trout and PowerPoint slides emphasizing the main points Professor Kennington wished to make about the research being conducted. Parker now understood better the nature of whirling disease and the approaches being taken to get it under control. So far, the main rivers of Yellowstone National Park had been spared from the disease while, in contrast, rivers not too far from the boundaries of the park, such as the Madison, Big Hole, Bitterroot, and Missouri, had been infected with the disease for several years. The impact on the local economy, which depended on the fishing business, had been severe, thus placing increased urgency on finding a way to either stop the advance of the disease or at least keep it at bay.

Exiting the auditorium, Parker looked for Bryson Haggerty. He didn't see him, and he didn't want to hurry outside to look in the parking lot, knowing that he would have to explain to Beth why he was in a hurry, which he didn't want to do. This evening shouldn't be about Edgar's death or Parker's suspicion of Bryson Haggerty, but rather one of enjoying a friendship with a charming and captivating woman.

Breaking the silence, he asked Beth if she would like to walk over to the Snow Lodge Café for ice cream or a piece of pie. "Do I have to have one and not the other?" she said, again with her eyes sparkling and a slight smile.

"You may have pie à la mode, if that is your choice," responded Parker. "But remember, the pieces of pie at Snow Lodge are quite large."

"Then we'll share a piece," she countered. "And I'll also have some coffee."

They sat in a corner booth, she across from him, and ordered a piece of huckleberry pie à la mode and two coffees. "I saw you looking toward the rear of the auditorium a few times during the lecture. Was there someone there you were wanting to meet afterward?" Beth asked.

"You are one perceptive woman," he responded. "I didn't think I had made it that obvious. Yes, there was someone sitting on the other side of the auditorium that I thought I might talk with after the lecture. But, he must have left before I had a chance to locate him."

"Would I know him?" she asked.

"Probably not," he responded. "He moved to West Yellowstone only a few months before I did and is a loner and hasn't been involved with any town or park events."

"I don't want to pry, but you were obviously wanting to talk with him," she said. "Was it about your business or a fly-fishing outing?"

"Beth, it really isn't important that I didn't talk to him," responded Parker. "I can talk to him some other time. No big deal."

He felt uncomfortable being evasive with Beth. Not a good way to impress her, but he didn't want to involve her in his suspicions of

Bryson Haggerty, at least not until he had more concrete evidence. Thankfully, the piece of pie and coffees arrived, and the conversation turned to what, if anything, the Park Service might do if whirling disease did hit Yellowstone National Park's rivers.

Feeling more comfortable with her by the minute, he decided on the spur of the moment to ask her about having dinner together later in the week. "Beth, would you be up for dinner and a theater production at the Playmill Theatre later in the week?"

"That sounds wonderful," responded Beth. "What evening did you have in mind?"

"How does Saturday night sound?" he responded.

"Sounds perfect," she said.

"Okay, I'll get tickets for Saturday night," he said. "Let's meet at the fly shop around 5:30, have dinner, and then go to the Playmill. The production begins at 7:30, I think, but I'll check and let you know for sure."

The Playmill Theatre was a fixture in West Yellowstone and a source of family fun and entertainment during the summer. College students from throughout the Rocky Mountain region came and prepared three different productions, which were presented on Tuesday through Sunday evenings, with a different production every two days. The students earned college credit for their efforts as well as a stipend. The theater was small and intimate, holding about seventy-five people with a stage within a few feet of the front row of seats. The students not only performed but also served as ushers, sold popcorn and soft drinks at intermission, and greeted the audience before and after the production.

Finding her keys in her purse, she unlocked the driver's door of her Tahoe and turned toward Parker. Not sure of what to say or do, he reached out and shook her hand.

"This was fun. Thanks for inviting me," he said. It was an awkward goodbye, and he felt foolish. She looked at him in a surprising way and then slipped into the driver's seat.

"Me too; I enjoyed it," she said. "If I don't hear from you before Saturday evening, I'll meet you at your fly shop around 5:30." She smiled, closed the door, and backed out of the parking place.

Ugh, he thought. What a dumb way to end the evening. Talk about feeling foolish. He sensed she had been waiting for something, probably not a handshake. A light goodnight kiss would have been appropriate. He wanted to be affectionate and not so cold. What was wrong with him? Why was he so hesitant?

He replayed the evening during the drive to his cabin. Was he dreaming, thinking that this friendship with Beth might become something more? She could certainly attract any eligible man she wanted, so why was she showing an interest in him? He admitted that he was fond of her and for more reasons than her beauty. Having been burned by his former wife, he had been telling himself he wasn't going to rush into any relationship with a woman without both eyes being wide open. But, Beth wasn't just any woman. He liked everything about her, and she kindled feelings in him that had been dormant for a long time.

The message light on his phone was flashing when he entered the cabin. The first message was from Jim saying that a shipment of new Sage fly rods had been delivered that afternoon and he had placed them on the display near the front of the store. The second message was from Karen Black indicating that she hoped he was okay and she would like to talk with him, although she gave no indication of what she wanted to talk about. Probably something about Laurie, thought Parker, or maybe Hal Gamby. The third message was from Bruce Perkins. He said that the results of the autopsy were back and showed that Edgar did not die from a heart attack or other natural causes. The autopsy showed Edgar had been poisoned with a poison causing paralysis, which resulted in his drowning. Bruce said Edgar's death was now officially ruled as a homicide. In other words, Edgar had been murdered. Bruce ended his message saying that the FBI would now be handling the investigation.

Chapter Seven
Memorial Day
Monday, May 25

Wrestling throughout the night with questions flooding his mind, Parker hadn't slept well. Edgar had been despised by many people, but did someone despise him so much that he or she would kill him? Murder wasn't something that most people contemplated, no matter how angry or upset they might become. Trying to guess what had been at work within the killer's mind had kept him tossing and turning throughout the night.

If disliking Edgar had played a role in his death, there were many who disliked him, even hated him, and so who among so many would be the killer if disliking him was the motive? And there was the poison. What was it, and how was it administered? The poison must have been slow acting since Edgar had been fishing by himself for a few hours after lunch, which meant the poison had to have been administered either during the morning before lunch or during lunch, allowing for a few hours to pass before it took effect. If the poison was administered during lunch, that could point to Dick, Jim, one of the other presidents, or even himself as being the killer, since they were the only people to make contact with Edgar during lunch. On the other hand, with so many people fishing the Firehole River on opening day for fishing in Yellowstone National Park, it wasn't out of the realm of possibility that someone approached Edgar while he was fishing and offered him a drink or a snack laced with poison. If it was someone Edgar knew, it would have been easy to approach him without suspicion and administer the poison. Then the poison would have been fast acting, causing instant paralysis.

Determining the poison was a key to finding the killer, he concluded. Until the poison was known, no conclusion could be made about who might have access to such a poison. Rat poison could be purchased across the counter by anyone, but it didn't cause paralysis. A more exotic poison probably required some type of a license or certificate, which might even be recorded in Gallatin County, assuming the poison was available locally. He had gotten up from bed at this point due to his tossing and turning and sat on the front porch in the rocker where he thought about Bryson Haggerty and his research in the area of poisons. Certainly, Haggerty knew how to get his hands on any number of poisons, and since he had a huge grudge against Edgar and had showed no emotion when Parker had told him of Edgar's death, he remained a top suspect in Parker's mind.

Another possibility was that Edgar knew the killer well enough to chat with him on the bank of the river or while standing in the river. Being friends, Edgar's suspicion of any unusual behavior by a friend would have been dismissed on the grounds of their friendship, and this would have enabled the killer to stick a needle into Edgar and inject the poison. Edgar would have collapsed being paralyzed, enabling the killer to hold Edgar's face under water long enough to cause him to drown. Once dead, the body could have been dragged into the trees where Parker found it.

Another possibility was that the poison had been placed in Edgar's water bottle that he carried in his fishing vest. If that was the means of administering the poison, any person attending the meetings at the Cutthroat Conference Center could have placed the poison in Edgar's water bottle while he was busy and wouldn't notice. Edgar said there were seven hundred presidents attending the meetings. Given this possibility, any of the seven hundred was a suspect.

Even though it was still early morning, he had called Bruce Perkins twice, each time leaving a message. Realizing it was a holiday—Memorial Day—he nevertheless assumed the Security Office would be open since this would be a day of high visitation within the park. He wanted more specifics about what poison had been used, approximate time of death, if Edgar's water bottle had been tested, and if any needle mark was found on his body. Also, he wanted to remind Bruce of Edgar's fly rod. It was still in the cab of his pickup. Now that the FBI was handling the case, he figured the fly rod should be given to the FBI. He also wanted to know the name of the agent assigned to the investigation. Since the nearest FBI office was located in Billings, he assumed the agent in charge would be from Billings.

He knew he was still a suspect, as were Dick and Jim, so the sooner he cleared all of them of suspicion, the better. Sooner or later, the news would get out that the owner and employees of the Gold Medal Fly Shop were suspects in a murder investigation. Such news could cause business to decline as customers shied away and went to the other fly shops. Clearing Dick, Jim, and himself of suspicion meant finding the killer, and he felt compelled to press ahead with his own investigation in spite of what Bruce Perkins had said.

Placing another call to Bruce Perkins, he had the same result: a voice-mail message. Bruce was probably already up to his ears with some disturbance between people arguing over a prime picnic spot or with someone running through an entrance gate without paying the entrance fee. Many of the one-time visitors to Yellowstone National Park didn't realize that the entrance fee was a real bargain. For $20, a person had access to the world's premiere national park for seven days with no additional charges for evening talks by rangers, campfire explanations of geology or the geysers, or use of the information centers or nature trails. Many of the visitors would spend more than $20 on food or fuel and never think twice about it, but paying a $20 entrance fee, which helped maintain the Park and keep it as a quality experience for future generations, seemed to be extravagant to some people.

He next called Beth Richardson. She too wasn't available, so he left a voice message.

"Hi, Beth, this is Parker. I wanted to tell you again how much I enjoyed last night, and I'm looking forward to dinner and the theater on Saturday. I also wanted you to know the results of the autopsy on Edgar Hickson showed he was poisoned. The FBI now has jurisdiction."

"Good morning." He turned to see Dick walk into the shop. "You are here early today," said Dick. "Couldn't sleep knowing today was Memorial Day, or was it the result of your date with Beth last night?"

Parker ignored the comment about his evening with Beth. "I had a lot on my mind, and I couldn't shake it," he responded. "I learned the results of the autopsy of Edgar's body. He was poisoned, which paralyzed him, causing him to drown. Bruce Perkins believes Edgar was murdered. Because of the strong possibility that he was murdered, the FBI is now handling the case."

"You're kidding, aren't you?" responded Dick. "Murdered? Poisoned? How? Are there any suspects?"

"You're asking the same questions that I had floating around in my head during the night," replied Parker. "Now you know why I didn't sleep much. I've placed three calls already to Perkins, but he wasn't available. I'm as curious as you are to learn more about the specifics of the autopsy."

The fly-shop phone rang, and Dick answered. He handed the phone to Parker and said it was a woman asking for him. "Hello, this is Parker Williams speaking."

"Mr. Williams, my name is Janet Van Kampen. I am an agent in the Billings office of the FBI. I have been assigned the Edgar Hickson case."

"Ms. Van Kampen, I was told by Bruce Perkins that the FBI now had jurisdiction over the case, so I'm not surprised to have received a call from you. Please know that I am available to help you in any way I can."

"Thank you, Mr. Williams. I have the file for the case, and this morning I've been familiarizing myself with its contents. The file says you knew Mr. Hickson well, and you were the one who found his body. I also see you were one of a few people who were with Hickson before he died."

"Yes, all that is true, and I would hope I could explain to you why I shouldn't be considered a suspect nor should either of my employees," responded Parker.

"Are you referring to Mr. Wells and Mr. Hill?" she asked.

"Yes, Dick Wells and Jim Hill," responded Parker. "Neither knew Edgar, and more importantly, neither had a motive to kill him."

"Mr. Williams, why don't we talk about this tomorrow morning; shall we say mid-morning?" she asked. "And I would also like to interview Mr. Wells and Mr. Hill at that time."

"That time is okay with me, and I'm sure it also will work for Dick and Jim," he said.

"Thank you, Mr. Williams. I'll see you tomorrow morning at your shop. One last thing, Mr. Williams. I have requested the assistance of the Gallatin County sheriff with some of the work of the investigation. You may expect to be contacted by the sheriff's department."

Hanging up the phone, a depressing thought crossed Parker's mind. What if the assistance of the Gallatin Sheriff's Department came in the person of Lt. Hal Gamby? Certainly, Sheriff Larson wouldn't assign him to a high-profile case like this was bound to be. This case had the potential of bringing quite a bit of publicity to the sheriff's department, and Hal Gamby was the worst representative the sheriff's department could assign.

He remembered he had failed to inform Agent Van Kampen about having Edgar's fly rod. Perhaps Bruce Perkins had told her, but wouldn't she have inquired about it and told Parker what to do with it if Bruce had told her? He called the number she had given him and her voice mail answered. He left a message telling her he forgot to tell her about Edgar's fly rod and that he could give it to her in the morning when she came to interview him.

For the remainder of the day, he waited on customers, thinking as he did about how Edgar could have been poisoned. Was it possible for someone to surprise Edgar and stick him with a needle? The noise of the flowing water of the river would cover any noise made by anyone wading from behind Edgar, thus, surprise was possible. On the other hand, sticking someone with a needle in the middle of a river that was wide open in terms of not being hidden from the view of cars passing on the road or other people fishing nearby, seemed far-fetched. More plausible was that the poison had been ingested by Edgar, either from the water in his water bottle or from something he either ate or drank earlier in the day. The more he thought about the difficulty of poisoning Edgar, the more he became convinced that Edgar must have ingested the poison, probably when he drank from his water bottle. Testing Edgar's water bottle was critical, and he needed to make sure Agent Van Kampen didn't overlook doing it.

Chapter Eight
Tuesday
May 26

Enjoying his morning cup of Starbuck's coffee on the cabin porch, Parker watched the morning light from the rising sun moving downward on the Madison Mountain range to the west. The purple glow of the mountain peaks and rocky crags contrasted with the dark-green hue of the pine-covered sides of the mountains. The morning was still with only the sound of birds serenading each other breaking the silence of the crisp air. Today would be a chamber of commerce day with a blue sky, low humidity, a slight breeze, and a temperature in the high 70s.

When he awoke, he realized he hadn't done any fishing the past few days, contrary to what he had promised himself when he opened the fly shop. This morning, he had the itch to feel the throbbing of a rainbow or brown trout through his Sage fly rod. He decided to call Dick and tell him he wouldn't be in to the shop until later. Instead, he would drive to the Hebgen Lake dam and fish the Madison River just below the dam where good-sized brown trout inhabited the river. He wanted to lose himself in the joy of fly-fishing and, at the same time, forget about the murder of Edgar Hickson, if that was possible.

Several boats dotted Hebgen Lake as he drove Highway 20 toward the dam and the beginning of the Madison River tailwater. The lake was like glass, allowing the mountains surrounding it to be reflected in the water, reminding him of paintings and photos he had seen in museums and art galleries in the East. People crammed into the cities along the eastern seaboard could only look at paintings and photos and dream of what was his to see every day. Along the road were various visitor information signs and dioramas describing the earthquake of 1968 that had devastated the area and created Quake Lake. The earthquake had caused the side of a mountain bordering the Madison River to break away, triggering a monstrous slide of rock, dirt, and trees, which in turn created an earthen dam blocking the flow of the river. The backed-up river rose more than one hundred feet, creating an overnight lake and causing campers in a nearby campground to scramble to high ground where they were eventually rescued by a helicopter. Dead tree trunks still rose above the water line like a company of sentinels as stark reminders of the awesome power of Mother Nature.

Pulling into the small parking area downstream from the Hebgen Lake Dam, he saw someone fishing immediately below the dam. Normally, he wouldn't have given this person much thought as there was more than enough fishable water for both of them without either encroaching on the other's area. It was the hat being worn by the person that caught Parker's attention. It was unusual in that it wasn't a typical hat worn by a fisherman. Fishermen in the West usually wore a cowboy hat or a straw hat with a wide brim to protect them from the intense sun at the higher altitude. The hat this fisherman was wearing was an African safari-type hat with one side rolled up and tied to the other side by a rawhide string across the top of the hat. He had seen only one hat like it since arriving in West Yellowstone, and it wasn't worn by a tourist. This hat either was the same one or a close resemblance to the hat that Bryson Haggerty was wearing when Parker had spotted him entering the Gray Wolf Pharmacy.

Opening the glove compartment, he took out his binoculars and focused on the person. Sure enough, it was Bryson Haggerty. Remembering how jittery Haggerty had been in the pharmacy and how he tried to avoid Parker when Parker asked him if he had heard about Edgar's death, he wondered if Haggerty knew that Edgar had been murdered. If he did, he certainly would react differently to being told people knew it was a murder than if he thought people believed Edgar had died from natural causes. He had been fishing the Firehole River on Saturday, so he certainly could have been fishing close enough to Edgar to approach him without Edgar becoming suspicious. If Parker only knew the poison that had been used to kill Edgar, he could confront Haggerty with that information and watch his reaction. Even without knowing the poison, he decided to confront him anyway. The news of Edgar's death being a murder might produce a reaction, although he didn't know what reaction he hoped Haggerty would show.

Pulling on his chest waders, he grabbed his fly rod, stepped cautiously down the riverbank, and entered the river well downstream of Haggerty. He didn't particularly want to sneak up on him, nor did he want to leave him with an easy escape route. Of course, if he did bolt upon seeing Parker, that would only add to the suspicion that Parker already harbored. Since it would be much more difficult for Haggerty to wade upstream against the current if he was going to attempt to avoid Parker, Parker knew he had the advantage as he was cutting off the most logical and easiest escape route.

He was within fifteen yards of Haggerty when Haggerty realized someone was approaching from behind. He turned, and for a second, Parker saw a look of fear cross his face. Why the look of fear, thought Parker, unless he is worried that I know something he doesn't want me to know. "Good morning, Bryson. How's the fishing?" asked Parker.

"Good," responded Bryson. "I've caught several browns on a #6 stone fly nymph."

"So, the browns are interested in stone fly nymphs this morning," said Parker. "Thanks for the tip. I hope I'm as fortunate and get into some nice browns, too. Say, did you hear that Edgar Hickson was murdered?"

"Murdered. No, I hadn't heard that," responded Bryson, who seemed to stiffen as he talked. "No matter how he died, as far as I'm concerned, he got what was coming to him."

"He was poisoned," responded Parker. "The FBI is now involved. The FBI lab in Denver is analyzing the poison to determine what it is."

"The FBI? Why the FBI?" Bryson moved closer to Parker as he talked.

"That lab in Denver is quite the place. It should be easy for them to find out what poison was used."

Parker again saw him stiffen and his face redden. "If you're wondering if I had anything to do with his murder, let me spare you the effort of asking me any more questions. While I despised the man and am not sorry that he is dead, I didn't kill him nor do I have any idea who did. Now, if you don't mind, I would like to fish that eddy line just behind where you are standing."

"Bryson, I'm not implying anything by my questions," said Parker. "I thought you would want to know Edgar was murdered. Aren't you curious about the poison that was used? After all, your research area is poisons, isn't it?"

"You know that I do research with poisons," responded Bryson. "Is it a crime or something?" Bryson was now becoming defiant, almost bordering on belligerent. "No, I'm not curious about the poison that killed Edgar. Anyone can purchase poison over the counter that can kill someone. Like I told you, I'm glad he is dead. The world is a better place without him. I didn't have anything to do with it, and I'd appreciate it if you wouldn't ask me any more questions."

"One last one," said Parker. "Have you been contacted by the FBI?"

"No, why should I be?" Bryson was now shouting. "How many times do I have to tell you, I know nothing about any of this."

Parker could see that the conversation had ended. He turned and waded downstream, careful to avoid wading through the eddy line Bryson had pointed out. At all times, regardless of who the other person might be, fishing etiquette prevailed among serious fly-fishers. You simply didn't wade through the water another person was fishing or getting ready to fish.

Haggerty was holding out, hiding something; Parker could sense it. The momentary look of fear suggested he was hiding something that he feared Parker might know. Did he know more about Edgar's death than he let on? Parker couldn't put the pieces of the puzzle together. What motive for killing Edgar did Bryson have besides disliking, even hating, Edgar? Many other people disliked Edgar, including Parker himself. Was disliking or even hating someone motivation for murder? He realized he needed to do research into Haggerty's background if he was going to put the pieces of the puzzle together and clear Dick, Jim, and himself of suspicion. In the meantime, he was wasting good fishing time.

Bryson said he had been successful with a #6 stone fly nymph. Parker reached into his vest pocket and then opened his fly box labeled "large nymphs." He couldn't believe it, no #6 stone fly nymph. Worse yet, he had no stone fly nymphs of any size in his fly box. What kind of a fly-fisherman was he, to go to the Madison River without some stone fly nymphs in his box? He better not let Dick, Jim, or any of the guides know about this. They wouldn't let him forget about it for a long time.

He settled on a #8 pheasant tail nymph. It wasn't a stone fly nymph, but he hoped the trout wouldn't be that particular as to notice the difference. If the trout were that particular in what they were eating, he would know soon enough. He waded over to where several boulders broke the surface, causing the water to cascade around them. The diversion of water around the boulders created some natural feeding lanes for the trout to take advantage of while staying out of the more rapid current. He studied the water and saw no activity on the surface of the water. If there were trout in the vicinity of these feeding lanes, they were feeding subsurface. If that was happening, his nymph should get some action.

He placed two split-shot on the tippet about two feet above the fly. He didn't change to a sinking tip line like some fly-fishermen would do. Using a floating line and adding weight in the form of split shot worked well, and it also saved him the time of changing fly lines back and forth. He didn't use a strike indicator since he didn't believe that a strike indicator added anything to his fishing success. Some people swore by them, but he did fine without one. His ability to detect the strike of a fish taking the nymph wasn't diminished without using a strike indicator.

Casting across and slightly upstream of the boulders, he allowed the fly to drift with the current. The secret was to have the nymph drift like a natural insect would drift in the current, and as the fly reached the point where all the fly line allowed on the water was played out, the fly would swing in an arc across the current until it was nearly completely downstream. It was during this arc that trout often would strike.

On his third cast, he felt a slight thump as the fly neared the end of its sweep through the arc. Setting the hook, he felt the pulsation of a fish trying to shake itself free of the pressure caused by the pull of the line. This was an area of common misunderstanding, which he often had to explain to clients he was guiding. A hook does not cause a fish pain. When a fish fights, it is not because of the hook but because of the restriction of its ability to move freely due to the pressure that is applied against the fish by the pulling of the line. He caught a glimpse of the crimson-streaked silvery side of a rainbow trout catapulting out of the water while continuing to shake its head. A good seventeen or eighteen inches of fighting trout was on the end of the fly line, he guessed. A rainbow here in brown-trout water. This was one of the joys of fly-fishing, having the unexpected occur.

For ten minutes, the rainbow made several runs upstream interspersed with leaps out of the water, only to have Parker give line when it was needed and reel in line when constant pressure was required. Not wanting to overtire the fish, he applied more pressure and reeled it in. Probably sensing the fight was over or due to exhaustion, the rainbow came willingly to the net. Reaching into the net, which remained in the water for the protection of the fish, he extracted the barbless hook from the upper lip of the fish. A good seventeen plus inches was his educated guess as he gently released the trout.

The best therapy for him, thought Parker. Fly-fishing, even when no fish were caught, was very therapeutic. The beauty of the surroundings and the sounds of nature, instead of machine or man-made noises drowning out the senses, brought a feeling of wellness and contentment. He caught and released three more fish, two brown trout and a whitefish, in the area of the feeding lanes defined by water rushing by the boulders.

Driving back to West Yellowstone, he stopped at his cabin to check his voice messages. There were two. The first was from Beth telling him that she had received his message about Edgar's death being a murder. She was shocked and wanted to talk with him more about it. She also said she too had enjoyed their evening together and was looking forward to dinner and the production at the Playmill Theatre. The second message was from FBI agent Janet Van Kampen reminding him she would be interviewing him in the morning, when she would also pick up Edgar's fly rod.

STONE FLY NYMPH

Hook:	Heavy bent nymph hook (e.g., Mustad 37160, #2)
Thread:	3/0 black monocord
Tail:	Moose body hair
Body:	Dark-brown wool with a small strand of dark-cream wool
Ribbing:	Stripped peacock herl
Thorax:	Dark-brown chenille
Hackle:	Dyed brown grizzly
Case:	Moose body hair
Feelers:	Moose body hair

1. Tie a bunch of black moose hair with butt ending halfway up shank of hook. Secure tightly with thread.
2. Divide tail into two equal parts.
3. Tie two brown- or amber-dyed goose quills to body.
4. Twist strands of cream wool yarn and brown wool yarn together to form one strand.
5. Wrap yarn to form body.
6. Wrap goose quills forward, ribbing tapered body.
7. Tie off goose quills.
8. Tie on medium bunch of dark moose hair.
9. Tie in medium brown chenille.
10. Tie in one or two brown grizzly hackle.
11. Lacquer thorax liberally.
12. Wrap brown chenille, forming thick thorax.
13. Wrap brown grizzly hackle forward. Tie off.
14. Wrap thread back from eye toward moose hair.

15. Trim top hackle over thorax.

16. Pull moose hair forward, forming case.

17. Wrap forward and tie down remaining moose hair, forming full thorax.

18. Trim bottom and side hackle.

19. Lacquer case, body, and tail liberally.

PHEASANT TAIL NYMPH

Hook:	Nymph hook
Tail:	Four cock ringneck pheasant tail fibers
Body:	Same pheasant tail fibers wrapped on hook shank
Ribbing:	.005" diameter copper wire
Wing:	Same pheasant tail fibers pulled over the top
Legs:	Pheasant tail fibers
Thorax:	Peacock herl over layers of copper wire.
Thread:	6/0 brown

1. Cover hook shank with tying thread. Tie in strands of pheasant tail fibers for the tail.

   Tie in a piece of copper wire 5–6" long. Tie in a second bunch of pheasant tail fibers for body.

2. Wrap pheasant tail fibers forward and tie off. Rib it with copper wire and tie off.

3. Tie on a section of pheasant tail fibers for the case.

4. Tie on two strands of peacock herl.

5. Wind three or four layers of copper wire to form a heavy thorax.

6. Pull peacock herl fibers forward and tie off with thread. Wrap thread backwards to the middle of the hook.

7. Wrap peacock herl backwards. Tie off with thread.

8. Advance thread forward. Wrap peacock herl forward.

9. Pull pheasant tail fibers forward and tie off.

10. Pull pheasant tail fibers backwards into two equal bunches. Wrap thread backward to secure legs. Whip finish and trim.

The pheasant tail nymph can be modified to become a "beadhead" by adding a gold-colored bead to the head of the hook.

Chapter Nine
Wednesday
May 27

Parker awoke early. Before slipping off to sleep, he had remembered a friend who was now employed at the university where both Edgar Hickson and Bryson Haggerty had once worked at the same time. Reaching over to the nightstand, he picked up the phone and placed a call to his friend and former colleague president, George Manheim. George had recently resigned as president of Upper Tennessee State University, trading his position as president for a faculty position as professor of chemistry at Western Tennessee State University. Since the time in Tennessee was two hours later than in Montana, Parker knew he had to call before 6 AM Montana time to have a chance of talking with George. He was curious if George knew, or could find out, what had occurred to cause Haggerty to be so bitter toward Edgar.

His call was answered on the second ring. "Hello, George Manheim here."

"George, this is Parker Williams calling."

"Parker, well I'll be," said George. "Are you in Tennessee, or are you calling me from out where the deer and the antelope still play?"

"George, I'm here in my cabin in Montana. I hope you appreciate how highly I regard you to be making this call so early. It's only quarter to six here and even the deer are still asleep."

"Parker, I'm flattered. But you must have something important on your mind to be calling me this early, so you better get to it. I'm due to a meeting with the dean in a few minutes. While I would rather talk with you than that old windbag who should have cashed it in several years ago, there is a new assistant professor from the University of Oregon who will also be at the meeting, and I want to get the lay of the land with her, so to speak."

"I don't miss those types of worthless meetings I used to have to attend," responded Parker. "Let me tell you why I'm calling. I can't give you all the details in a short period of time, so if you do want to know more, call me back at your convenience, and I'll share what I can with you."

Parker told George about Edgar's murder, his finding Edgar's body, that Edgar had been poisoned, and how Bryson Haggerty was a suspect. "George, can you fill me in about Haggerty, especially about why he despised Edgar so much? Did he and Edgar have a major falling out? Did Haggerty ever make any threats toward Edgar?"

"I heard some things, Parker, but not enough to draw any conclusions," replied George. "I'll tell you what. I'll do some asking around and talk with some faculty members who were in the same department with Haggerty. They probably know a whole lot more than I do. You're right, something triggered the bad blood between Haggerty and Edgar. I'll get back to you in the next couple of days. Right now, I have to run to my meeting."

They said goodbye and Parker hung up the phone. If George could find out why Bryson Haggerty hated Edgar, perhaps it would help explain why he might have been driven to kill him. Parker would then be able to give some concrete information to Janet Van Kampen, which she could use to either obtain a search warrant to search where Haggerty lived or, if the information Parker could piece together made enough sense, arrest him on suspicion of murder.

Driving to West Yellowstone, his mind was filled with numerous thoughts about Edgar Hickson, Bryson Haggerty, Janet Van Kampen, George Manheim, Beth Richardson, and the Gold Medal Fly Shop. He felt guilty since he was devoting neither the time nor attention to the fly shop that it deserved, and while he could weather a financial downturn resulting from reduced business activity, he knew that Dick, Jim, and Laurie could not. He simply owed it to them to be more involved in the business. He vowed he would be, just as soon as he cleared Dick, Jim, and himself by finding the killer.

Stopping at the Three Bears Café, he wanted to grab a quick breakfast before going to the fly shop. He wished he hadn't. As he was waiting for his order of a short-stack of blueberry pancakes, Hal Gamby walked into the café and sat on the stool at the counter next to Parker. "Parker, were you surprised to learn that Edgar Hickson was poisoned?" asked Gamby. Parker realized that Janet Van

Kampen must have told him about Edgar being poisoned. "I bet you didn't know that I've been asked by Sheriff Larson to be available to the FBI to assist them in the investigation," continued Gamby. "So, you will be seeing more of me. By the way, Parker, where were you during the afternoon Edgar was murdered? You certainly could have killed him and then acted like you discovered his body a few hours later."

"Hal, you must be kidding," responded Parker, trying to maintain his cool. "You aren't so stupid as to accuse me of killing Edgar, are you? But, why am I even responding to your ridiculous questions? You're not the FBI, and as yet, you have no official role."

The tension between the two men was broken with the arrival of Parker's blueberry pancakes. He turned slightly on his stool so that his back would be toward Gamby, who, taking the hint, stood up from his stool and took a seat at a table across the café. As Parker gulped down his pancakes, without hardly tasting them, he was seething. The nerve of this guy. Accusing him of murder. He put down a $10 bill and quickly exited the café without a glance toward Gamby.

He had just enough time to go over the schedule for the day with Dick and Jim before a blue, four-door Ford sedan with U.S. government license plates pulled in front of the fly shop. A woman stepped out of the driver's side dressed in black slacks, French-blue blouse, black vest, gray blazer, and wearing a minimum of jewelry. Her hair was sandy colored and cut short in a page-boy style. She had an overall attraction that he wouldn't say was stunning, but certainly more than merely appealing. She walked into the fly shop.

Parker greeted her and introduced himself. "Hello, I'm Parker Williams." He offered his hand.

Shaking his hand, she said, "Mr. Williams, I'm FBI Agent Janet Van Kampen. Thank you for being available to meet with me." Her handshake was warm but not domineering. "Is there a place we can talk in private?"

"Let me show you a room we have in the back," responded Parker. "It's full of boxes and fishing stuff, but it's private, and I think it'll work."

She walked to the room and looked in. "This will work fine," she said.

"Dick, please take over for me while I'm in the backroom," said Parker.

"Mr. Williams, do you mind if I use a recorder?"

"No, that's fine with me," he responded. She had one of those slim, new Panasonic digital recorders with voice-recognition capability. With voice-to-text conversion software, the intermediate step of transcribing was eliminated.

"Mr. Williams, please start at the beginning of the day on Saturday and tell me everything you can remember that happened. Please try to recall any behavior on anyone's part that seemed odd or contrived."

He described the events of the day ending with his discovery of Edgar's body and his telephone call to Bruce Perkins. She asked a few questions, but mainly allowed him to talk uninterrupted. Before he had finished, he told her about finding Edgar's fly rod.

"Where is the fly rod now?"

"It's in the cab of my pickup. I haven't touched it since I put it there. Should I go get it?"

"No, I'll get it before I leave," she responded. "It may be evidence, and I want the FBI crime lab to go over it." She asked him to verify the names of the presidents and guides that had been with or near Edgar on Saturday. She produced a list of names, which Parker verified. "There are FBI agents from communities near the universities where each is a president, and those agents are interviewing them. I want to interview Mr. Wells and Mr. Hill after we finish. Where might I find them?"

"Dick and Jim are scheduled to work throughout the day,"

"I'd like to interview them in this room, if that's acceptable with you," she said.

"Sure, no problem," responded Parker. "I'll tell them you're waiting for them."

"Is there anything else you want to tell or ask me, Mr. Williams?"

"Matter of fact, there is. Has anyone mentioned a fellow named Bryson Haggerty to you?"

"No, who is Bryson Haggerty?"

He told her about Haggerty and his conversations with him in the West Yellowstone Pharmacy and also yesterday morning when fishing the Madison River. "Where can I find Haggerty or at least contact him?" she asked.

"I don't know," responded Parker. She got up from the chair, indicating that the interview was over.

"I forgot to ask you, Mr. Williams, do you have any poisons here at the shop or at your home?"

"No. Why are you asking?"

"Please don't remove anything from your shop or your home without first contacting me."

"Agent Van Kampen, you're treating me like I'm a suspect. Am I?"

She smiled. "At this time, Mr. Williams, everyone is a suspect."

As they walked out of the backroom, he noticed that Dick was tying flies while Laurie and Jim were waiting on customers. "Agent Van Kampen, please meet Laurie Black, Jim Hill, and Dick Wells."

She proceeded to arrange interviews with Dick and Jim. Parker caught a look from her that he interpreted as asking him, "Who is the young woman? Why didn't you tell me about her?" She and Dick went to the backroom.

Parker had turned off his cell phone during the interview, so he turned it on and checked for messages. There was one message from George Manheim. "Laurie, Jim, I need to run a quick errand and pick up tickets at the Playmill Theatre."

When he was out of earshot of the fly shop, he hit the call-back button on his cell phone. After three rings, a woman answered, "Professor Manheim's office."

"This is Parker Williams returning Professor Manheim's call."

She said that Professor Manheim was available and she would put Parker through to him. "Hello, Parker?"

"Yes, George, it's me. Thanks for calling back."

"Parker, I hope I caught you on your way to the Henry's Fork or the Madison to do some fly-fishing."

"Sorry, George, not today. I did fish the Madison yesterday morning. Got into a nice pocket of seventeen inchers. Are you jealous?"

"You bet I am. Maybe I can get out there yet this summer or fall. But, we can talk about that later. Let me tell you what I learned about Bryson Haggerty and our recently departed friend Edgar Hickson."

"Fire away, George," responded Parker. "I'm anxious to hear what you learned."

"Bottom line, Edgar denied Haggerty tenure," said George. "The reasons given by Edgar were viewed by faculty, and even some administrators, as bogus. It created quite a stir because the department, dean, university tenure committee, and the provost all recommended Haggerty be awarded tenure. So, in denying tenure, Edgar stuck it in the face of all these people as well as Haggerty himself."

"Sounds like Edgar," responded Parker. "He certainly knew how to tick off everyone. So, what bogus reason did he give?"

"I was told that Edgar's reason was that Haggerty's research was in an area that was inconsistent with Edgar's vision for the university. Since he was president, he had the privilege, so he claimed, of saying that his vision was the correct one. Can you believe the arrogance of the guy, claiming his vision was the vision the university should follow? Anyway, the trustees didn't buck him, or maybe they never knew what was going on. So, Haggerty was denied tenure and thus had to leave the university."

"George, do you know if Haggerty's research area was poisons?" asked Parker.

"Yep; in fact, Haggerty had quite a reputation in the area of lethal poisons. It all went out the window when he was denied tenure. Get this. He also lost a very lucrative research contract when the funding source found out he had been denied tenure."

"That would certainly drive Haggerty to want revenge," replied Parker. "George, this is really helpful. I now understand what motive Haggerty would have to harm Edgar."

"Yeah, it certainly explains why Haggerty despised Edgar," responded George. "And, I was told that there had been a heated exchange between the two of them which had been overheard by several administrators. They heard Haggerty tell Edgar that he would pay dearly for what he had done. And, when Haggerty was leaving the university, he told his department chair that if he ever had the chance, he would kill Edgar. Plus, he said he knew a way he could get away with it."

Chapter Ten

After mulling over the conversation with George Manheim for two hours, Parker called Karen Black to ask her if she knew where Bryson Haggerty lived. Given her knowledge of the real-estate market in West Yellowstone, she, more than anyone else, would be knowledgeable about where he lived. Sitting down on the bench in front of the Playmill Theatre, he took his cell phone and punched in Karen's home telephone number. It was the same as her daughter Laurie's number, which was in his cell phone's number book.

Laurie answered and recognized Parker's voice. She said she had been interviewed by Agent Van Kampen as had Dick and Jim. Parker could tell from the sound of her voice that she was upset. "Laurie, how did your interview go with Agent Van Kampen?" he asked.

"Why was I interviewed?" she responded. "I never knew Edgar Hickson, nor was I anywhere near the Firehole River last Saturday. Didn't you tell her all that?"

"Laurie, Agent Van Kampen never asked me about you. It never crossed my mind that she would interview you. I'm sorry. I guess I should have been thinking that she would interview everyone who was around the shop on Saturday morning. I should have told her that you weren't anywhere near Edgar."

"Well, it's okay," responded Laurie. "It's just that she is so official and everything. You know, the FBI. I've never been around an FBI agent before, and it is kind of intimidating, at least it was for me."

"Laurie, Agent Van Kampen is only doing her job. She is following the procedures established by the FBI, I'm sure. She has to interview everyone that was in the vicinity of Edgar that day. I'm sure she believed everything you told her. I doubt you will be bothered by her again. Is your mom home?"

"Yes, she is." Parker heard her call Karen and tell her he was holding for her.

"Parker?"

"Hi, Karen. I'm sorry that Laurie had to be interviewed by the FBI agent. I'm sure it was only a formality. There certainly is no reason for concern."

"Oh, she knows that," replied Karen. "I told her being interviewed by a real FBI agent is different than watching one interviewing someone in the movies. Now, what's on your mind?"

"Karen, would you know where Bryson Haggerty is living?" he asked.

"You know, Parker, Haggerty is a strange duck," she replied. "A loner, I'd say. Have you ever noticed his shifty eyes? I have told Laurie several times, watch out for a man with shifty eyes."

"Yes, he is strange acting at times," responded Parker. "How about it, do you have any idea where he is living?"

"Well, he came into the office right after he arrived in town and asked about cabins to rent. He said he didn't want to live in town. He preferred to be in a remote area by himself. I gave him the rental-listing book. He wanted to see a cabin out behind Fisherman's Village, so I gave him the directions, and he came back in a few hours and said he would take it. I contacted the owner and negotiated a month-to-month rental agreement for him. Haggerty said he didn't know how long he would be staying in the area. Usually owners want at least a six-month lease, preferably a year, but this owner was somewhat desperate, so the month-to-month arrangement was acceptable. Haggerty paid the security deposit and first month's rent in advance, and I haven't seen or heard from him since. I have no idea if he is still living there."

"When did this all happen?" he asked.

"A few weeks after you arrived, as I recall," she responded.

"So, sometime in late April, about a year ago?"

"Yes, right around then, as I recall."

"Can you give better directions than behind Fisherman's Village?" he asked.

"I never went out there myself, so I can't be too sure," she replied. "I might still have the description that was used for the real-estate listing. I don't have it here, but if you want to meet me at the office, I can see if I still have it."

"That would be great," he said. "What time would work for you?"

"I was just going to finish something here and then go to the office, so maybe in fifteen minutes."

"See you then, Karen, and thanks." He dialed information and asked for the telephone number of Bryson Haggerty. The automated information system responded that there was no listing for that name. Perhaps Haggerty only used a cell phone. More and more people were doing that in lieu of a home-based telephone.

Jeff Waggoner was working the ticket booth in the Playmill Theatre as Parker requested two tickets for the Saturday evening production of *Annie Get Your Gun*. "What's the latest about the murder?" asked Jeff. "Any suspects yet?"

"How do you know about the murder, Jeff?" asked Parker.

"Come on, Parker, you know that in a small town like this, news travels fast, especially news out of the ordinary, and a murder is certainly out of the ordinary around here. If this were New York or Los Angeles, no big deal. Happens every day in those places. But here ... it is big news."

Parker didn't feel like getting into a conversation with Jeff, especially about Edgar's murder. "Really haven't heard much, Jeff. The FBI has taken over the investigation. I guess we won't hear much until they have found the killer or killers. Thanks for the tickets."

Back at the fly shop, he noticed Laurie waiting on two customers wanting to schedule a float trip the next day on the Madison River. Dick was at his vise tying flies, and Jim was rearranging merchandise to hopefully make it more appealing to customers eager to part with some money. Since it wasn't too busy and the least busy part of the day was just beginning, he wouldn't be missed if he walked over to Black's Real Estate Agency. Hopefully, Karen had kept the listing of the cabin Haggerty had rented, and Parker would be able to obtain directions from the listing.

Entering Black's Real Estate Agency, he saw Karen staring at a computer screen in the back of the room. "Parker, I found that listing. I'm printing it right now. The directions aren't the greatest, but I think they are good enough for you to use. Say, why do you want to find Haggerty's cabin? He is weird, you know."

Pulling out a sheet of paper from her printer, she walked over to Parker and handed it to him. He caught the scent of her perfume, and he looked at her with a more discerning eye. She really was an attractive woman, in fact, very attractive. He wondered what had been behind her divorce. She certainly was always pleasant with him, and she had the looks to go along with her personality.

"Thanks, Karen. This place of Haggerty's is quite a bit off the beaten path. I'm not surprised. Just the place he would want, given his desire to be alone."

Saying goodbye, he headed back to the shop. If it wasn't too busy, he would drive out to Fisherman's Village and try to locate Bryson Haggerty's cabin. If Haggerty was there, Parker wasn't sure what he would do. He could confront him with the information he had learned from George Manheim, but he wasn't sure he should tip him off that Parker considered him a prime suspect in Edgar's murder. Better that he tell Janet Van Kampen what he had learned and allow her to deal with Haggerty. "Dick, can you, Jim, and Laurie take care of things here for a little while?" he asked. "I need to run an errand. It shouldn't take too long. If you need me for anything, I'll have my cell phone with me."

"Sure, Parker, the three of us can handle things here," said Dick. "Take your time. We'll see you when you get back."

Backing out of his parking place behind the shop, he turned onto Madison Avenue and headed west out of West Yellowstone on Highway 91 toward Ashton, Idaho. Fisherman's Village was about nine miles west of West Yellowstone, just inside the Montana side of the Idaho and Montana state line. As he drove, he again thought about calling Janet Van Kampen. Maybe he should tell her what he was doing. He could also tell her the information about Bryson Haggerty and Edgar that George Manheim had told him. After he thought about it, he decided not to call her as he figured she would tell him to stop playing detective. She would probably tell him he was interfering with FBI business, and if he didn't heed her request and stop, he might make an enemy of Janet Van Kampen, and he certainly didn't want that. No, better to find Haggerty's cabin, see if he was there, and confront him if he was. He could then call Janet and tell her the information along with how Haggerty had reacted.

He turned in at the entrance to Fisherman's Village. The village, built in the late '80s, consisted of A-frames with cedar siding and faded green roofs. Dirt roads wound through the village, and snowmobiles and ATVs were parked hither and yon, giving the area the look of a transient population. He wondered why it was called Fisherman's Village since there was no fishing in the immediate vicinity. He would have to ask Karen Black more about the village. But if he were being honest with himself, he knew he really wasn't as interested in learning more about Fisherman's Village as he was in talking again with Karen Black. There was something about Karen he found alluring. But, what about Beth? Was he losing interest in her and gaining interest in Karen? He shook his head as if to dislodge any more thoughts about these two women. They were occupying too much of his thoughts.

Following the directions on the real-estate sheet Karen had given him, he drove along a dirt road that wound behind the east side of Fisherman's Village and into the lodgepole pine forest. The road narrowed and became more rutted as it entered into a stand of lodgepoles, which, he suspected, continued for several miles as part of Teton National Forest. At a fork in the road about one mile past Fisherman's Village, the directions said to take the left fork. It was only two worn down, tire-width paths. After another mile of bouncing and jostling, he saw a cabin appear in a small clearing that had been cut from the lodgepole forest. According to the real-estate listing, this was Bryson Haggerty's cabin. There were no vehicles parked around the cabin or any signs of activity. Parking his pickup in a spot obviously used for parking, he opened his door and listened. Only sounds of the forest greeted him.

As he began to walk toward the cabin, he froze. He realized he had nothing with which to defend himself or ward off a watchdog. While he didn't believe in carrying a gun, he did own one, but right now it was locked in a cabinet in his bedroom. The gun was registered, and he had a permit to carry it, so why hadn't he thought of taking it along with him? Now that he knew where Haggerty lived, he could go back to his cabin and come back with his gun for protection. After all, if Haggerty had killed Edgar, he wouldn't hesitate to kill again. A chill went up his spine. But all this time, only the sounds of the forest were heard. No barking of a dog. No indication of any activity in or around the cabin.

He told himself to get a grip. Haggerty wouldn't be so stupid as to kill him. When he didn't return to the fly shop, Dick would wait for a while, then try to find him, and it wouldn't take long to put two and two together. In a town as small as West Yellowstone, Karen Black would certainly tell about giving Parker directions to Bryson Haggerty's cabin, and it would be only a matter of time until Haggerty was found and charged with two murders … Parker's and Edgar's.

When he reached the door of the cabin, he knocked. No response. No dog barked or growled from the inside. He knocked again. Still no response. He tried the door. It was locked. Walking around to the back of the cabin, he knocked on the back door. Same response … silence. This door too was locked. Fortunately, he was tall enough to look in the windows. Unfortunately, all but one of the windows had blinds that were drawn. From the one window where the blinds weren't drawn, he could see what appeared to be some sort of a laboratory. Bottles, beakers, mixing dishes, what he thought to be a centrifuge, and a variety of pipits and small glassware were scattered across a countertop. Must be where Haggerty does his work with poisons, he thought.

So much for confronting Bryson Haggerty. Walking back to the pickup, he wondered if Haggerty had already fled the West Yellowstone area. He berated himself as he thought that by confronting Haggerty the other day when they were fishing the Madison River, Parker inadvertently had tipped him off that he was a suspect. Haggerty may have decided to flee the coop without gathering up anything from the cabin. He could already be out of the country. And, if he had pre-planned Edgar's murder, he could have a forged passport with a different identify and money wired into an offshore bank. In other words, Bryson Haggerty might be gone for good.

Chapter Eleven

Pulling up to the fly shop, Parker saw Janet Van Kampen's blue Ford parked in front. She must be inside the shop, he thought. Good. He could tell her what he had learned about Bryson Haggerty and seen at his cabin.

Entering the fly shop, he saw only Laurie. "Laurie, is Agent Van Kampen around?" he asked.

"She's in the backroom with Dick and Jim," responded Laurie. Laurie looked rather sheepish. Wondering what had been going on, he walked to the backroom and knocked on the door. Janet Van Kampen opened it, holding her Panasonic recorder as well as her notebook. Dick and Jim were sitting on boxes across from her while in the corner, with a smirk on his face, was Hal Gamby. Parker groaned inwardly. What was he doing here? Janet Van Kampen must have invited him.

"Agent Van Kampen, I have something very important to tell you. Earlier, I left a voice-mail message for you, but I'd prefer to tell you now."

She smiled, and her body language seemed to convey a message of "Relax, don't overreact to what I'm going to say." He hoped he read her correctly. "Mr. Williams. I realize you left me a message, but I haven't been able to listen to it yet. I'll be finished here in a few minutes, and then we can talk."

He closed the door and went back to where Laurie was straightening the display of fishing reels in the display case below the main counter. This display case was always locked as these reels were small enough to be easily picked up and placed in a pocket if they weren't under lock and key. With the price of some of the reels in excess of $300, losing only a few to shoplifting quickly put a dent in the bottom line in terms of profits.

"Laurie, how long has Agent Van Kampen been here, and was Lt. Gamby with her when she arrived?" Parker asked.

"She came about forty-five minutes ago and first asked for you. I told her you were gone but would probably be back soon. She then approached Dick and Jim and asked if she could talk with them."

"How about Gamby, was he with her?"

"No, she called him from here and said she wanted him to join her interviewing Dick and Jim."

The door to the backroom opened. Dick, Jim, and Janet Van Kampen walked out. Parker could sense some tension, and he wondered what questions she had asked. He also wondered why Hal Gamby hadn't come out of the backroom. What was he doing in there by himself? Being careful to keep Dick and Jim separated from Parker so that conversation among them was impossible, Janet walked up to Parker. "I can talk with you now if this time works for you," she said.

"Works for me, and I do have some important information for you, which I prefer to tell you in private."

Without acknowledging what he had said, she turned around and walked to the backroom. It was obvious she expected him to follow, which he did. Before entering the room, he said, "Will Lt. Gamby remain while we talk?"

"Lt. Gamby has been designated by the sheriff's office to assist with the investigation," she responded. "He will participate in those aspects of the investigation where I feel he could be of assistance."

"With all due respect, Agent Van Kampen, I don't believe he can be of any beneficial assistance in your investigation, and, in particular, I don't think he should be party to our conversation."

"With all due respect to you, Mr. Williams, I'll decide when and how Lt. Gamby will or will not participate in this investigation, not you."

He decided to let it rest and make the best of the situation. Following Janet into the room, he saw Hal Gamby sitting on a box in the corner. "Hello, Hal."

"Good to see you too, Parker," replied Gamby. "I assume Agent Van Kampen told you of my selection to be involved with this investigation. Now I'm official."

Parker could see the smirk on Gamby's face grow more intense. He's loving this, thought Parker. He thinks he's playing in the big leagues and is able to lord it over everyone. "Yes, she has, Hal. Congratulations. The more minds we have devoted to finding the killer of Edgar, the quicker the killer will be apprehended." Parker almost choked as he said these words.

"Correction, Parker. The more expert minds we have, not amateur minds like yours," replied Gamby.

"Mr. Williams, you had something you wanted to tell me?" Janet Van Kampen asked. "Go ahead; let's hear it."

Knowing that everything he was about to say would be heard by Hal Gamby, be spread by him throughout the sheriff's department and from there throughout the community, Parker hesitated. Maybe he should try to dodge this by saying it really wasn't anything now that he had time to think about it. But he knew she would press him, and he also knew she would probably catch him in a lie trying to cover a previous lie. Then what credibility he did have with Janet Van Kampen would be shot. So, he decided to tell it all and let the chips fall where they might.

He went through the entire story of learning about the problems between Edgar and Bryson Haggerty from George Manheim and how Haggerty had said that if he had the chance to kill Edgar, he would. He described how he had driven out to Haggerty's cabin and saw the makeshift laboratory with what he assumed were poisons. He ended by telling them that Haggerty had the motive, means, and opportunity to kill Edgar.

Watching Janet's face as he relayed the information to her, he saw no indication of her feelings or thoughts. Either she was good at covering her feelings or she found Parker's information to be so-so and not very helpful. "What I don't appreciate, Mr. Williams, is your going off on your own and freelancing," she said. "May I remind you that you remain a suspect in this case. Maybe your gallivanting around playing Sherlock Holmes is your attempt to throw us off onto some wild goose chase. The FBI is in charge of this investigation, not you. You are an amateur at best, and you could easily get hurt by doing this amateur sleuthing. If you don't back off and stay away from any further involvement in this investigation, I won't hesitate to place you under house arrest. Is that understood?"

Parker could see the smile on Hal Gamby's face during this dressing down. It was a contemptuous smile that Parker knew meant, "Hey, dummy, you've really ticked her off. Better back off now, or you will get your butt kicked, and I would love to do the kicking." She interrupted his thoughts. "Now that we understand each other, I've a question for you. What do you know about the University of Colorado Health Sciences Center in Denver?"

"I've heard of it, but I've never been to it," answered Parker. "I do know it is one of the top health-related research centers in the country, and it brings in beaucoup bucks in federal grant money."

"Did Edgar Hickson ever talk to you about the Health Sciences Center?" she asked.

"No, Edgar never mentioned anything to me about the Health Sciences Center."

"Are you sure?"

"Yes, I'm sure. Why do you ask?"

"Your name, the word *strong*, and the acronym UCHSC were found on a note among Hickson's personal belongings in his room at the Cutthroat Conference Center," she responded. "Do you have any idea why he would have such a note in his room, or why your name is on the note?"

"Sure don't. I have no idea why my name would be on a note in Edgar's room, other than he did call the shop about scheduling the fishing outing so possibly he wrote my name down to remind himself to make the call," responded Parker. "What did the note say?"

Janet looked at Hal Gamby, and then gave Parker a quick look, which told him she was making up her mind whether she would answer his question and if she would, if she would do so with Gamby in the room. Looking directly at Gamby, she said, "Lt. Gamby, would you please step out of the room for a few minutes? I'd like to talk with Mr. Williams alone."

Parker could see Hal Gamby's face turn red as he realized he was being shut out of what might be some important information. Was this a sign that Janet didn't trust Hal Gamby, or had the two of them planned this in advance as a bad cop/good cop maneuver to get Parker to open up more? By the look on Gamby's face, it seemed not to be planned between them. He appeared shocked, and then, as he realized what was happening, the shock turned to anger. "Wait a minute," Gamby said. "I'm as much a part of this investigation as you are. I need to be here to hear everything."

Assuming a posture that conveyed a sense of authority, she responded, "Lt. Gamby, may I remind you that I am in charge, and this is my investigation. You have been invited to assist me, and I decide when I need your assistance. For now, your assistance has been completed. Thank you. I will be contacting you when I need your assistance again." As she said this, she opened the door, indicating that the conversation was over and he was to leave.

Hal Gamby shuffled out with a not-so-pleased look on his face. Parker was tempted to flash him a "who's in the doghouse now, buddy" look, but he decided to let good enough alone. After Hal Gamby was out of earshot, she closed the door and turned to Parker. "Look, I don't like him any more than you do. My superiors in Denver decided to allow the sheriff to have a piece of the action for public relations purposes. I would appreciate it if you didn't blab it around how I stiffed him. I'd like to keep my job, at least for a while."

He noticed a twinkle in her eye. She was enjoying this. How should he play this good turn of events? For now, he would play it straight and see where it led or she took it. "I must tell you, Agent Van Kampen, I sure do feel more comfortable without Hal Gamby around. I'm sorry you got stuck with him."

"Thanks, but I can handle him," she responded. "Now, let me tell you about the note. It might trigger something in your memory." She flipped a few pages in her notebook. Parker surmised she had written down verbatim what had been written by Edgar on the note. "Written on the note was the name Parker, the word *strong*, and also UCHSC. A computer search determined that UCHSC stood for University of Colorado Health Sciences Center. We figure "strong" refers to strength. What we don't know is why your name was on the note."

Parker knew he had to answer thoughtfully, as he was a suspect and every word he said would be scrutinized. "I don't know why my name is on the note. As I said, Edgar may have written my name when he called me about the fishing outing. He could have used the note to jot down people or places he needed to call, and thus, there isn't any connection between any of what is on the note. All three items could have been randomly written."

"I thought of that too, Mr. Williams." She crossed her arms and walked to the door. Parker thought she would open it. Instead, she turned and said, "If you do remember anything related to why your name might be on the note along with the University of Colorado Health Sciences Center or the word *strong*, you call me. I also asked your employees about the fly that was attached to the tippet and leader of Edgar's fly rod. The lab report showed traces of a toxic poison—tetraodontoxin to be precise—embedded in the fly. According to the autopsy, this poison matches the poison found in Edgar's body."

"So, the poison that killed Edgar was on the fly he was using, do I have that correct?" Parker asked.

"Yes, I assume that the fly was the source of the poison that paralyzed Edgar and led to his drowning," she responded. "I understand this fly came from your fly shop. What can you tell me about how and when this fly came into Edgar's possession?"

"The fly was one Dick gave to Edgar. Dick had tied a Royal Wulff fly for each president as a gift from the fly shop. He gave each president a fly at the end of lunch. I don't think anyone else handled the flies, certainly not while he was tying them. I also doubt if anyone handled them after he finished tying them until he actually gave them to the presidents. To think that Dick put poison on the fly given to Edgar is ridiculous. Dick didn't know Edgar, nor did he have a motive to kill him. He had nothing to gain from Edgar's death. He didn't kill Edgar any more than Jim or I did. You're wasting your time considering any of us as suspects."

She looked at him with a look that conveyed a sense of frustration. "Mr. Williams, please, I'm not accusing you, Jim, or Dick of anything. I'm only trying to determine how the poison may have become embedded in the fly. Someone had to have access to the fly long enough to spread poison onto it, and all three of you were close enough to the fly to have done it."

"None of us did anything to those flies. I'm certain you will find that out when you find the source of the poison. And the note in Edgar's room, I'm really confused about it."

"Now, Mr. Williams, as far as what you or I say to anyone, let's agree that we have agreed to leave the investigation to me and Lt. Gamby. You aren't going to play Sherlock Holmes anymore. I will follow-up on the information you gave me about Bryson Haggerty, and I hope to have some information back on that by tomorrow afternoon. In the meantime, don't discuss any of this with anyone, and please don't leave the area without telling me."

Chapter Twelve
Thursday
May 28

Parker woke up with a start. He had been dreaming, but he couldn't remember any of the dream. Funny how your mind worked. One minute things were so real, you could see, feel, and hear them, and then, poof, entirely gone from your memory. Throwing back the flannel sheet and stretching, he heard the blue jays arguing among themselves just outside his window. One of the area's most prolific birds, blue jays seemed to have a sense of when their bickering back and forth would be most annoying to humans.

He entered the bathroom and began to brush his teeth. As he was brushing, it hit him. Why hadn't he thought of this before? A college friend was a professor of biochemistry at the University of Colorado Health Sciences Center. Carl Turner and he had lived in the same dormitory for two years at Alma College in Michigan. Carl had graduated with honors and gone on to the University of California at Berkeley where he earned his PhD in biochemistry in five years. Parker had lost track of him after Berkeley, but a recent invitation to attend an Alma College class reunion had listed Carl as being a professor at the University of Colorado Health Sciences Center. Carl might be able to help make some sense of what Janet Van Kampen had told him about the note found in Edgar's room and also possibly shed some light on a connection between Edgar and the Health Sciences Center. It was a long shot, he realized, but nothing ventured, nothing gained.

As he was getting dressed, he thought of Hal Gamby. Had he gone to Sheriff Larson and told him how Janet Van Kampen had brushed him off? If he had, Sheriff Larson may have contacted Janet and read her the riot act. On second thought, Parker doubted it. Janet was, after all, an FBI agent, and telling an FBI agent off wasn't a smart thing to do unless you were an FBI agent yourself. Even if Hal Gamby had told Sheriff Larson, he had probably been told to forget it and stay out of Janet's way. Couldn't happen to a nicer guy, thought Parker. He could still see the smirk on Hal Gamby's face when Parker had first seen him with Janet in the backroom of the fly shop.

After taking the box of Oatbran cereal down from the cabinet over the refrigerator, he added some fresh blueberries to it in a bowl and poured skim milk over it. Cereal with fruit for breakfast was still one of his favorites. Looking at his watch, he saw that it was still early. With no compelling reason to get to the shop early, he decided he would fish the Gallatin River just outside Yellowstone National Park. The stretch of the Gallatin River he liked to fish was only about fifteen minutes from his cabin, being twelve miles north on Highway 91 toward the Big Sky Resort. This stretch of the river caught the early morning sun, which usually triggered an early morning hatch of blue dun insects. If he was fortunate, he would have some marvelous dry fly action for a couple of hours. After fishing, he would drive a few more miles further north to the Big Sky Resort and talk with Gene Durbock, the manager of the Cutthroat Conference Center, where the meeting of the presidents had been held. Parker wanted to inquire if anything unusual had occurred during the meeting of the presidents, or, if he were lucky, someone might remember if any unusual behavior had been exhibited by any of the presidents that comprised the group that had been together for the fishing outing. Perhaps one of the conference center staff had seen or heard something that would have a bearing on Edgar's death or the note found in his room.

He had thought long and hard about talking with Durbock since Durbock was viewed as an extremist for his insistence that historical documentation existed showing that Jim Bridger, the famous explorer credited with discovering much of Yellowstone National Park, had obtained several deeds to portions of the park, which, if true, meant that descendants of Bridger were entitled to compensation from the federal government in lieu of the land that had been taken by the federal government for the park. Durbock also insisted that he was a descendant of Bridger and would host a press conference during a forthcoming meeting of the Yellowstone Coalition to release documentation proving his personal relationship as a descendant of Bridger. However, Parker's desire to learn if anything had happened at the meeting of the presidents that would throw some light on the murder of Edgar had won out and prompted him to plan to go to the conference center to talk with Gene.

The headwaters of the Gallatin River lie in the upper northwestern section of Yellowstone National Park. The river flows north out of the park for nineteen miles through both open meadows and canyon walls until it joins the Jefferson and Madison rivers at Three Forks, Montana, to form the Missouri River. Parker planned to fish the section of the Gallatin River immediately outside the park where the river meandered through a small meadow area resulting in deep pools and undercut banks. Parking his pickup in the pull-off area where tourists entering the park from the north often stopped to take photos of the "Welcome to Yellowstone National Park" sign, he glanced toward the river and saw dimples breaking the surface of the water. The fish were taking some insect that was floating in the surface film of the water. Pulling on his waders, he picked up his fly rod and walked slowly to the river's edge.

Taking care to make sure his shadow didn't cross where the fish might be holding, he entered the water. Reaching into the water with his homemade insect catcher made of cheesecloth, he found blue dun insects in the surface film. He opened his fly box that contained imitations of insects that often were found floating in the surface film of water and took out a #16 imitation of a blue dun and proceeded to tie it onto the 5x tippet at the end of the fly line. In fly-fishing fashion, he wet the portion of the tippet that would be tied to the fly by passing it over his lips and tongue. He wanted saliva on the tippet when he pulled the knot tight to tie down the fly. Any fly-fisher worth his or her salt knew to do this since, if it wasn't done, the strength of the tippet would be compromised. Many a large trout had been lost when the tippet broke due to it losing much of its strength because it hadn't been "licked down" with saliva prior to the knot being tied.

Positioning himself downstream and across from where the fish were probably holding, he spotted fish waiting for the current to carry the floating insects into their feeding lanes. His first cast was somewhat short. He did not pick up the fly and fly line immediately, but allowed the fly to drift well past the area where the trout where holding. Only then did he pick up the fly and fly line from the water, making sure there was no chance of spooking the fish. He recast, and this time he had judged the distance accurately. The fly drifted only a few feet when it was sucked into the mouth of a fish. Setting the hook, the fish responded by shaking its head as it jumped out of the water. He saw the red stripe down the side of the fish set against the glimmering silver body. A rainbow trout, and a good-sized one. He guessed it to be eighteen to nineteen inches. For the next ten minutes, the rainbow and he had a standoff.

He fished for two more hours, catching and releasing six more fish—four rainbows and two browns. As the sun rose higher, the presence of the floating insects diminished until none were visible. Switching to a #14 soft hackle peasant tail nymph, he continued to catch fish, which had gone deeper in the water to feed on nymphs. At about 9:30, he went back to his pickup, peeled off the waders, carefully broke down the fly rod, and placed it in its aluminum tube. No sense snapping off the delicate tip by catching it in a closing door or by jamming it against the side of the pickup.

He drove the few miles up the Gallatin River canyon to the turnoff to the Big Sky Resort and the Cutthroat Conference Center. The conference center had been a large project that had taken more than two years to complete. It had all the amenities of a first-class conference facility behind the rugged Western look, which emanated from the natural log exterior. A huge lobby, with a natural rock fireplace dominating the middle of the lobby, greeted him. Bison, elk, and antelope heads were tastefully arranged along the natural paneled walls. Prints of Remington, Russell, and Rey originals were hung throughout the center with accent lighting in all the proper places. A large picture window on the west wall framed Big Mountain, the ski mountain of the Big Sky Resort. He could certainly understand why the presidents' association had chosen to have its spring meeting at such an elegant place in such a magnificent setting.

He stopped at the front desk. "Is Gene Durbock available?" he asked. "I'm a friend, and if he is around, I'd like to say hello."

"I'll see if Mr. Durbock is available," said the young woman behind the desk. "Your name please, sir?"

She punched a number on the telephone console that had so many buttons and lights that Parker wondered how anyone knew which button to push for what purpose. In only a few seconds, another young woman, dressed in a Western outfit with all the trimmings, approached him. She had a light-green cowboy hat, matching neckerchief tied around her neck, silver belt, light-green boots, and a silver studded vest. "Mr. Williams, I'm Vicki Cushing,

Mr. Durbock's executive assistant. If you would come with me, Mr. Durbock has some time and would like to see you."

As they walked across the lobby and up the stairs at the far end to the mezzanine, Parker asked her how long she had been Gene's administrative assistant. "Since the center opened last year," she answered.

"Have you worked for Gene since you arrived?" Parker asked.

"Yes, and I certainly am fortunate to be able to work with such a kind man," she replied.

"Miss Cushing, do you remember the recent meeting of the presidents' group? Were you involved with them during their meetings?"

"Yes, I remember them. Some of them sure thought highly of themselves—rather snobby if you ask me."

He wanted to ask her if she remembered any of the individual presidents and especially those of the fishing group, but before he could, she opened the door to a suite of offices. She escorted him to an office at the end of the hallway where Gene Durbock was waiting with a broad smile on his face. "Parker, good to see you; it's been awhile," Gene said.

"Gene, same here," responded Parker. "Quite the place you have here."

"Yes, isn't it something? I think it may be the most luxurious conference facility in the entire northern Rocky Mountain region. It obviously isn't for those looking for a low-budget facility. Our main calling card is for upscale conferences and corporate retreats."

Vicki excused herself while Gene and Parker brought each other up to date in each of their lives. As Parker anticipated, Gene told Parker of his intention to hold a press conference at a forthcoming meeting of the Yellowstone Coalition to release documentation regarding his claim to be a descendant of Jim Bridger and therefore entitled to compensation from the federal government. Parker finally got around to asking Gene about the recent presidents' meeting. "Gene, did you observe or hear about any unusual behavior by any of the presidents during the meeting?"

"I do remember the group, about seven hundred presidents of universities as I recall," responded Gene. "But, I wasn't around them very much. I concentrate on the management of the center and usually don't mix with the guests. I leave a lot of that smoozing stuff to Vicki, especially with the male guests. They like to have a good-looking woman dote on them. Let's see if she might be able to help."

Gene pushed a button on his telephone. Parker heard a buzz in what was probably a room adjoining Gene's office. "Yes, Mr. Durbock," Vicki said as she stepped into the office.

"Vicki, Parker asked me about the recent meeting of the university presidents we had here last weekend," said Gene. "He wondered if I had seen any unusual behavior or heard any unusual talk among the presidents. I told him I don't get involved very much with our guests, but that you might be able to help."

"Well, I did spend quite a bit of time around the presidents, especially during the initial cocktail hour," she replied. "As I told Mr. Williams, presidents of universities are different. I guess they are used to being pampered and waited on, so the staff went out of their way to try and be available to them. What, in particular, Mr. Williams, were you asking about?"

"To be honest, Vicki, I can't be specific. Maybe shouting or excessive ridiculing between presidents. Did you happen to be around President Edgar Hickson, for instance, and did he exhibit any peculiar behavior toward other presidents?"

Vicki blushed at the mention of Edgar. "Well, Mr. Williams, I'm not sure how to say this, but I did come to know President Hickson. Not that I wanted to, you understand, but he, ah, he, ah … made a pass at me which was rather direct, if you get my point. I did tell him to bug off and mind his own business, but you know what he did? He smiled and said to me … oh, the audacity of the man ... he said that I didn't know what I was missing. I'm sorry, Mr. Durbock. I didn't egg him on or anything. I'm so embarrassed."

"Vicki, I'm sorry this happened; you have nothing to be ashamed about," responded Gene. "Parker, it sounds like this Hickson guy is quite the dude."

"Vicki, I too am sorry you had such an experience," said Parker. "I must say that I'm not surprised that Edgar would act like that, but that isn't an excuse. I'm sorry you had to endure it. Do you remember anything else about President Hickson, about him interacting with any of the other presidents?"

"Well, after he was so obnoxious and direct with me, I really tried to avoid him. But, I do know that at the social and cocktail hour the first evening of the meeting he kept talking loudly and laughing, especially, it seemed, at the expense of a few of the other presidents."

"Vicki, do you remember anything more about this loud talking and laughing?" asked Parker. "Do you know who the other presidents were? Do you remember what President Hickson said?"

"Mr. Williams, I hope you understand, this was the first social and cocktail hour of the meeting, so I was focusing on making sure the service was prompt and the food and beverage tables were being restocked. I really wasn't engaged in any conversations or listening that closely to conversations."

"Vicki, neither Parker nor I are questioning your work ethic or your commitment," said Gene. "You know how pleased I am with your work. You are a model employee. I certainly couldn't function nearly as well without you. Anything you might recall about the conversation by President Hickson might help Parker. Think hard. Maybe you can recall something."

"Thank you, Mr. Durbock," she replied. "As I said, this was the first social and cocktail hour of the meeting. The presidents were renewing acquaintances and friendships, meeting new people, and generally engaging in small talk. President Hickson was with three or four other men. I overheard him saying something like: "Are you strong again? How about being strong again? Being strong again would certainly be a surprise, wouldn't it?" All the time he was laughing and, I guess I would say, being rather obnoxious. It was like he was baiting the person to whom he was talking. I'm sorry; I don't remember much of anything else."

"So, Edgar was, in your judgment, baiting one of the presidents?" asked Parker. "Do you have any idea what this was all about or who the other president was?"

"I'm sorry; I don't remember other things being said or whom the other president could be. I do remember that I saw one of the food tables running low on stuffed mushrooms, so I went into the kitchen to check. When I came back from the kitchen, I didn't see President Hickson again."

"Vicki, thank you. You really have been most helpful," said Parker. "If you remember anything else that involved President Hickson, please either give me a call or share it with Gene. He will then get in touch with me."

After Vicki left, Gene and Parker talked about how Parker's fly shop was doing and about getting together to fly-fish the Gallatin River. Gene also gave Parker a personal invitation to attend the press conference during which he would release his documentation related to his claim to be a descendant of Jim Bridger and entitled to compensation for the land that the federal government illegally took from Bridger for Yellowstone National Park.

Parker thanked Gene and asked him to again thank Vicki. As he headed back to West Yellowstone, he mulled over in his mind what Vicki had said. It sounded like a classic putdown of someone by Edgar. The fact that the note found in Edgar's room included the word *strong* and the conversation that Vicki described included the word *strong* seemed more than coincidental. What did it mean? What was its connection, if any, to the University of Colorado Health Sciences Center or, for that matter, to him?

The key to figuring all this out might lie with the inclusion of the University of Colorado Health Sciences Center on the note, he thought. Did any of this have anything to do with Edgar's murder? He told himself not to be distracted. Bryson Haggerty was still the top suspect. Haggerty had a motive, the knowledge of poison, and the opportunity, since he was fishing the Firehole River the same time Edgar was on Saturday. As for some of the presidents, sure they didn't like Edgar any more than everyone else, but what would be their motives? What did any of them know about poison and where would they obtain it? These questions continued to play in his mind as he parked his pickup behind the fly shop.

BLUE DUN

Hook:	"Dry fly"
Tail:	Dark moose hair fibers
Body:	Dubbed grey muskrat fur
Wing:	Medium blue dun hackle tips
Hackle:	Medium blue dun saddle or neck hackle
Thread:	Pre-waxed gray

1. Tie on four to eight strands of dark moose hair. Tail should be length of hook.
2. Separate guard hairs from grey muskrat fur.
3. Attach muskrat fur to thread using thumb and forefinger to roll on.
4. Using thumb and forefinger, roll back and forth, rolling fur on thread.

5. Wrap fur forward. Taper extra fur when necessary to complete body.

6. Take two blue dun hackle tips and tie on.

7. Straighten hackle tips and bend them forward.

8. Tie on two more hackle tips.

9. Wrap hackle to wing. Pull back on hackle including wing and wrap forward.

10. Tie off thread to form head. Whip finish and lacquer.

11. Straighten hackle tip wings with finger.

Chapter Thirteen

Business in the fly shop had slowed down considerably with the passage of Memorial Day. In a few weeks, summer vacations for families with school-aged children would begin, but until then, business would be slow. Only one customer was browsing the fishing clothes when Parker entered the shop. Laurie was behind the counter organizing credit-card charges, Dick was tying flies, and Jim was in the backroom opening boxes, labeling contents, and placing the various items in the appropriate displays. Parker again felt grateful for his employees. He knew the fly shop would quickly go under if he didn't have employees like these three.

Looking through the inventory of wading boots and shoes, Parker heard his cell phone ring. The readout indicated the call was from Beth Richardson. "Hello, Beth."

"Hi, I'm in town … at the Three Bears," she replied. "I just ordered coffee and a piece of huckleberry pie. I wondered if you would be able to join me. I have to be over at Grant's Village to give the evening ranger program on the geology of the park, so I'm only in town for a little while."

While she was talking, he formed a mental image of her in his mind. How beautiful she is and how feminine, he thought, such a combination. He also remembered how much he had enjoyed their time together at the lecture on Tuesday evening. "You bet, Beth. I'll be right over. Save me a bite of pie … if you can withstand the temptation to eat it all before I get there."

"Then you better hurry," she said. "Huckleberry pie is too great a temptation to have around."

He told Laurie he was going over to the Three Bears Café to meet Beth. Laurie smiled. He thought he saw that look in her eye that women seem to get when they know something romantic was on the verge of happening. What is it with women? he thought as he walked out of the shop and headed down Madison Street toward the Three Bears Café. Women always are thinking that romance is on the minds of a man and woman when they meet at the drop of a hat. Laurie's smile seemed to be saying, "You're falling for her, and I know it, even if you don't."

"I see you saved me a couple of bites," he said as he slid into the booth opposite Beth. "Your ability to withstand temptation is obviously greater than mine." Immediately after saying it, he wished he hadn't. She could easily interpret his comment as sexually suggestive.

"Oh, I wouldn't be too sure about that," she responded, giving him a wink as she did. He was thrown for a loop by her comeback. He didn't know whether to keep up this flirtation or switch the subject. Fortunately, he didn't have to decide as he was saved by the presence of the waitress asking if he cared to order.

Ordering coffee, he asked if huckleberry pie was still available. "Sorry, the lady has the last piece," the waitress said. "We still have blackberry, cherry, and apple left if you'd care for any of those."

"A piece of blackberry, please," he responded.

"My second favorite fruit pie," said Beth. "Here, you finish the huckleberry, and I'll have a bite or two of the blackberry. So, tell me what you have been doing the past two days. Any more information about Edgar's murder or who his killer might be?"

He wondered how much he should tell her. He trusted her, but he didn't want to jeopardize their relationship by talking only about Edgar's murder. "Do you really want to know?" he responded. "I don't want you to feel that all we can talk about is what I'm doing or, in particular, Edgar Hickson's death. I want to know more about you, your job, your interests, and your hopes and dreams." As he finished, he cringed inside. His ears started to ring. You idiot, he said to himself. You might as well have said, "Let's be more than friends." Now you have really blown it.

What happened next gave him a feeling he hadn't experienced since his former wife and he were dating and into the first year of marriage. Beth reached across the table and gave his arm a squeeze and rested her hand on his arm. She told him that she wanted very much to share those things and more about herself, and she wanted him to do the same for her, but to do so, they needed to be together more often than for a few minutes over coffee and pie or for a few hours where most of the time was spent listening to a lecture. "But since neither of us can tell our life story nor describe our hopes and dreams in the fifteen minutes left before I have to leave for Grants Village, tell me the latest about Hickson's murder."

With the pleasant feeling still resonating within him, he cast all reservations aside. "I went to Bryson Haggerty's cabin and saw that he has a makeshift lab where I assume he works with poisons. You know, Beth, Haggerty had the motive to kill Edgar, and he was fishing the Firehole River the same time Edgar was. Seems to me he should be a prime suspect."

"I agree," she replied. "Has the FBI interviewed him or searched his cabin?"

"I don't know. I told Agent Van Kampen about Haggerty, and she was going to do some checking on his background, but I don't know what she found out. Another thing. Edgar wrote a note, which the FBI found in his room at the Cutthroat Conference Center, and it may provide a clue to his murder."

"A note. What did it say?" she asked.

"That's just it, it doesn't make any sense. My first name, the word *strong*, and the letters UCHSC were on the note. That's all there was. The FBI believes UCHSC stands for the University of Colorado Health Sciences Center in Denver. But, I can't figure out what connection there might be among my name, the word *strong*, which the FBI assumes means strength, and the University of Colorado Health Sciences Center."

"Yes, that is strange," she replied. "Now you've got me thinking too. You're sure there wasn't anything else written on the note?"

"I'm going on what Agent Van Kampen told me. And, one more thing, Beth, I visited with Gene Durbock and Vicki Cushing at the Cutthroat Conference Center. Vicki told me she overheard Edgar speaking loudly at a cocktail hour in the presence of other presidents. She said she heard him using the word *strong* several times and something about being strong again. According to her, he was getting a big kick out of doing it, like he was gibing one of the other presidents."

Beth looked at him with a questioning look. "What do you make of the note and the information Vicki provided?"

"I haven't been able to make any connection at all. Maybe there is a connection; maybe there isn't. Perhaps Edgar wrote those things down at various times, and there isn't any connection between them at all. That's my guess."

"I'm thinking about what you just said," she replied. "The word *strong* could have been written at random and have no connection to anything. The University of Colorado Health Sciences Center, that exists, but what it might have to do with Edgar, I don't get. And your name, that doesn't make sense either. Instead of searching for a connection, I'm with you about Bryson Haggerty. He is certainly a plausible suspect, especially when I tell you that he was seen by Winston Burk, the ranger working the southern entrance station, exiting the park early yesterday morning. Winston said the back of his truck was full of stuff, which Winston couldn't see because of a tarpaulin covering it."

"What?" Parker exclaimed. "Are you sure Winston saw Haggerty, not someone else? I wonder if Janet Van Kampen knows about this."

"I am only telling you what Winston told me at a meeting of rangers last evening at Mammouth Headquarters. He said he had heard about Edgar's murder and that Bryson Haggerty might be considered a possible suspect, so when Winston saw Haggerty heading out of the park, he thought he should make a note of it and tell someone. I think he told Bruce Perkins. Bruce may have told Agent Van Kampen."

Beth looked at her watch. "I have to be going," she said. "But I think you should think more about the word *strong* on that note. I know that the obvious way to look at it is in terms of "strong" meaning strength, but maybe it has nothing to do with strength. Maybe it is another person's name. Maybe it is the name of an organization or business. I'm wondering if "strong" was capitalized. If it was, it could indicate a proper name of someone, an organization, a clinic, or something other than referring to strength."

She again reached across the table and squeezed his arm. "Thanks for meeting me. I'm sorry I have to run. And let's not wait too long until we tell each other our life story and our hopes and dreams. If we don't touch base until Saturday, I'll meet you at the shop a little before 5:30. Bye."

He thought he had said goodbye and that he would see her on Saturday evening, but he wasn't sure if he had mumbled something or what he precisely had said. He didn't know if he was more affected by her presence and her overture that she wanted to be more than friends, or the fact that she may have figured out a piece of the puzzle of Edgar's murder. He had never given it a second thought that the word *strong* might refer to something other than

strength. But, if as she said, "strong" was capitalized on the note, then referring to another person, organization, business, or place called Strong were possibilities.

Taking out his cell phone, he called Janet Van Kampen. After four rings, her voice mail asked him to leave a message and said she would return the call. "Agent Van Kampen, this is Parker Williams. I need to ask you a question about the note found in Edgar's room. Also, did you know that Bryson Haggerty was seen exiting the park yesterday morning? Maybe he's trying to get away."

The Three Bears Café wasn't busy, so he didn't feel the pressure of having to give up the booth to waiting customers. So much had transpired in the short time he was with Beth that he needed some time to sit and try to sort it out. Better yet, he needed to do a list of what he knew, what he didn't know, who were suspects and why, and what he yet needed to find out. He took his napkin and began to write.

KNOW	DON'T KNOW
Edgar killed by poison	What poison and how administered?
Poison on Royal Wulff fly.	How poison got onto the fly and when?
Edgar probably wrote note including the word *strong*, the University of Colorado Health Sciences Center, and Parker's name.	Connection, if any, among the three?
Edgar talked about "strong" in the presence of some presidents.	What did he mean by "strong"? Was he directing this at a particular president? If so, whom?
The word *strong*.	"Strong" mean strength or refer to person, organization, etc.?
Bryson Haggerty knows poisons, had access to poisons, had motive and opportunity. Left the area quickly.	Only coincidental? Proof of any wrongdoing?

It was obvious that there was more he didn't know than he did. Feeling he had exhausted the avenues available to him to find the answers to his "don't know" items, he decided he either needed to do some work in the fly shop to get his mind off things or go fishing. Janet Van Kampen could find the answers. After all, she had the resources of the FBI behind her, and he had nothing.

Walking back to the shop, he continued to think about Beth. When his former wife walked out on him, he had promised himself he would avoid ever again having a deep relationship with a woman. For more than a year, he had kept his promise. He hadn't come across a woman, until now, to whom he had given more than a second look. Everything now seemed to be changing. He was growing fond of Beth, and he wanted to be around her.

Entering the fly shop, he saw Dick at his fly-tying bench. Parker marveled at how deftly and quickly Dick could turn a pile of feathers, hair, thread, chenille, and other materials into an exquisite fly that looked like the natural insect. "Did Laurie and Jim take off for lunch?" Parker asked.

"Yeah, things in here were slow this morning, so I suggested they not hurry back," responded Dick "I suspect they will be back in an hour or so."

"It looks like you're tying some Royal Wulff flies," said Parker. "Are these going to be the same as the ones you tied for the presidents or different?"

"I'm using the same materials I always use, so these should be the same. I know I was a little more careful tying the ones I gave the presidents since they were a gift, and I wanted those to be really well tied. I remember I was sort of put out that I ran out of barbless hooks before I could finish those. I had to tie three with barbed hooks, steel-colored hooks at that, and I also had to mush down the barbs, so those three weren't quite the same as the three with the gold barbless hooks."

Parker thought back to the Royal Wulff flies given to the presidents and to the fly he saw tied to the tippet on Edgar's fly line. Something stuck in his memory. "Wait a minute, Dick. You tied some of the Royal Wulff flies using barbed hooks that were steel-colored and the others using gold barbless hooks?"

"Sure did," responded Dick. "I remember because I was counting on all of them being tied with gold barbless hooks, and when I ran out after only three, I was bummed out."

"Do you remember to whom you gave the flies tied with the gold barbless hooks versus the flies with the steel-colored hooks?" asked Parker.

Dick looked off as if he was concentrating on trying to remember. Turning to Parker, he said, "I remember. I wanted the two women to each have a gold barbless one. You know, a little classy looking for the women. I thought your friend should get the other one, him being your friend and all."

"You mean President Edgar Hickson?" asked Parker.

"Yeah, President Hickson," responded Dick. "The two of you knew each other, so I figured that you would probably prefer he have the fly with the gold barbless hook. The flies with the steel-colored hooks, where I mushed down the barbs, I gave those to the other three presidents."

"You mean the other men presidents?" asked Parker.

"Yeah, that's right," responded Dick. "The other three men."

Chapter Fourteen

Parker had the feeling that Dick had just provided an important clue, but he didn't know how or what it might mean. Walking to the backroom and closing the door, he forced himself to try to bring into his mind the image of the Royal Wulff fly he saw attached to the tippet on Edgar's fly line. Was the color of the hook gold or steel? Forcing his mind to concentrate, he tried to will it to bring clearly into focus the fly and the color of the hook. The image that came into his mind was a Royal Wulff fly tied on a steel-colored hook.

If he remembered correctly and the Royal Wulff fly with which Edgar had been fishing was one with a steel-colored hook, then Edgar's original fly had been switched for another. Dick said he had given Edgar a fly with a gold-colored barbless hook, not a steel-colored one. Dick also said the flies with steel-colored hooks had been given to the other three men presidents. This would mean that one of the flies given to the three men presidents had been switched with Edgar's fly, and if this was true, it could mean one of the three men presidents was the killer. There was still the matter of obtaining the poison and putting it on the fly and also how Edgar had ingested the poison, but this could probably be explained once the color of the hook of Edgar's fly was clearly identified. One of the men presidents could have switched his fly for Edgar's fly during the ride in the van back to the Firehole River after lunch the afternoon of the fishing outing, or the switching could have been accomplished during lunch at the Fountain Flats picnic area.

Realizing he had to make sure of the color of the hook, Parker was determined to get another look at that fly himself or have Janet Van Kampen describe it to him. If it was the latter, he knew she would ask why he wanted to know. He didn't want to tell her his suspicions, at least not yet. There was still the question of how the poison got from the fly into Edgar's blood system, although he had a pretty good idea how that might have happened. The bigger question had to do with motive. What reason would one of the men presidents have for killing Edgar? Did one of them dislike Edgar so much that he would kill him? It seemed unlikely that disliking someone, no matter how great, would cause a person to commit murder. There had to be something else, some other reason. Edgar could have done something to one of them, or there might have been something Edgar knew about one of them that was so devastating that the person felt he had to kill Edgar. Another piece of the puzzle had to be within reach, but what was it? What did Edgar have on one of the men presidents, or what had Edgar done to one of them that was so horrific that one of them would kill Edgar?

Thinking again about what Beth had suggested about the word *strong* referring to a proper name, a name of a person, organization, business, or something other than meaning strength, he knew he needed to find out if Edgar had written "strong" with a capital S. Also, he wanted to contact his friend Carl Turner at the University of Colorado Health Sciences Center and determine what, if anything, he might know.

Deciding to take a few minutes for lunch, he turned to Jim who was busy cleaning the glass on the lower portion of the counter display case. "Jim, where did you and Laurie have lunch?"

"We went to the Lodgepole Pine Grill." The Lodgepole Pine Grill was a newcomer to West Yellowstone, and Parker had yet to have a meal there. He had heard good things about the grill's soups and sandwiches. "The special today is buffalo pot roast," continued Jim. "It was tasty and a nice portion. They probably get the buffalo meat from Ted Turner's herd up in Paradise Valley."

"That sounds good," replied Parker. "I think I'll try it. Hope they have some left. Are you and Laurie okay here with the shop for a little while?"

"Sure," responded Jim. "It shouldn't be too busy this afternoon. I suspect traffic will pick up Friday for the weekend. We already have three float trips scheduled for Saturday and two more for Sunday."

Even though the Lodgepole Pine Grill was on Gibbon Avenue about seven blocks west of the shop, Parker decided to walk. Blue sky, with an occasional white puffy cloud and no wind, meant you couldn't get a more perfect day than this one, he thought. Walking by the Bank of West Yellowstone, he was reminded that he needed to see Diane Milford, the loan officer of the bank. He needed to talk with her about possibly refinancing the loan he had taken to buy the fly shop. Interest rates had recently declined after Alan Greenspan had given Congress one of his eyes-glazing-over speeches about the economy. The next day, the Federal Reserve Board had lowered the prime rate ¼ point. Doing some calculations in his head, he had come up with a savings in monthly payments of nearly $300.

Entering the grill, he was taken aback to see Janet Van Kampen and Hal Gamby in a booth near the rear. She spotted Parker and gestured for him to come over. "I was hoping to see you a little later today," she said. "But since you are here, how about joining us for lunch? We haven't ordered yet."

Hal Gamby didn't appear to share her willingness to have Parker join them. The feeling was mutual. If Parker dared, he would have suggested Gamby get lost or she and Parker go to another booth. "Sure. Jim told me buffalo pot roast was the special today," Parker responded. "That sounded good to me, so here I am." He slid into the booth next to Hal. This way, he wouldn't have to look across the booth at him and could, in a sense, ignore him.

"We were going over the facts of the Edgar Hickson case and determining what the next steps should be," Janet said. "There are some missing pieces in the puzzle, and I want to get aggressive and pursue finding those pieces."

Parker thought this might be his chance to learn if Janet remembered the color of the hook of Edgar's Royal Wulff fly and if the word *strong* on the note found in Edgar's room was capitalized. As he was deciding whether he would ask her, she said, "You left a voice mail for me. I was going to stop by the fly shop after I finished lunch with Lt. Gamby and see what was on your mind."

With this opening, he decided to go for broke. If she accused him of meddling but let it go at that, he would say he was only curious about the hook and the word *strong*. If she pressed him to the point where he was forced to tell her about going to visit Gene Durbock at the Cutthroat Conference Center, he could tell her Vicki Cushing's story of how Edgar had behaved and what she had overheard him say. Telling Janet all this increased the probability that she might follow through on her earlier threat, but he felt he had to take the chance.

"I had two questions which I hoped you could answer," he responded. "I think both may have a bearing on who killed Edgar. I know you told me to stop sleuthing and to not interfere with your investigation, so let me say up front that I don't think I'm interfering, at least I don't feel I am." He could feel Hal Gamby tense up next to him. Gamby was probably waiting for Janet to lower the boom on me, and I know he would relish Janet berating me, thought Parker. Gamby most likely would chime in the minute he heard Janet unleash her criticism of Parker. But, she didn't seem upset, nor did she react at all. Instead, she responded calmly.

"Okay, it isn't that we're making fast progress on this case so that I can ignore any possible new evidence or theories. I haven't felt that you've been interfering, so let's hear what you think might have a bearing on the investigation."

Parker wanted to act like a child and turn and stick his tongue out at Hal Gamby and do the na-na-na-na-na-na routine. Since Janet was giving him some slack and also running a risk, he decided to play it cool. If neither the color of the hook nor the capitalization or non-capitalization of the word *strong* led anywhere, he knew that Gamby would find a way to report to Janet's superiors about the slack she was giving Parker. A reprimand or even a possible demotion for her might result.

"Agent Van Kampen, can you remember the color of the hook on the fly attached to the tippet on Edgar Hickson's fly line? In particular, can you remember if it was steel or gold colored?"

Indicating he was bored with the entire exchange and wanting to communicate his feelings to Janet, Gamby let out an audible sigh. Unfortunately for him and fortunately for Parker, she either didn't hear it or chose to ignore it. "No, I don't remember the color of the hook," she replied. "What do you think is the significance of the color?"

"Keep in mind the fly was tied by Dick Wells," said Parker. "He remembers giving Edgar a Royal Wulff fly tied with a barbless gold-colored hook. He also gave the two women a fly tied with a barbless gold-colored hook. However, he gave each of the other men presidents a Royal Wulff fly tied with a steel-colored hook."

She looked at Parker with a puzzled look that told him she might not be following what he was saying. "Okay, so what's the significance of the hooks?" she asked.

"I remember the fly on the tippet on Edgar's fly line was tied using a steel-colored hook, at least I think I recall that it was steel colored. If my memory is accurate, one of the men presidents may have switched flies with Edgar, giving him a fly which might have been doctored with the poison that paralyzed him."

Janet hesitated for a few seconds as she apparently thought about what Parker had said. She then looked across the booth directly into his eyes. "Interesting theory, Mr. Williams. It would be one piece of the puzzle that has escaped us, how the poison was applied to Edgar's fly. I surmised all along that the poison was added to the fly after Mr. Wells gave it to Hickson. This required getting the fly away from Hickson, adding the poison, and giving it back to Hickson, all before he tied it onto his fly line. I also thought that perhaps the poison was added to the fly after Hickson tied it on his fly line. This would require taking the fly rod away from Hickson for the time it took to add the poison to the fly and then returning the fly rod to him. Either way seems very unlikely in the presence of at least four other people."

Parker wanted to respond, but he saw she was thinking and would most likely want to outline her thoughts with him before he responded. "On the other hand," she continued, "if the flies were switched, as you think they may have been, it would be relatively easy to pull off in the presence of other people. As I understand, people who fly-fish are always playing around with flies, handling them, looking them over, and sharpening the hooks. So, no one would think it unusual for someone to handle his or her own fly."

"What about putting the poison on the fly?" said Gamby. "Wouldn't someone see that and wonder what was going on?"

Parker welcomed Gamby's comments, not because of what he said, but because it broke the tension that Parker could feel closing in on him. Parker quickly answered. "It would be easy and taken in stride by anyone. The poison could have been placed into something like a dry fly flotant bottle. The Royal Wulff is a dry fly meant to float on the surface of the water. A flotant is usually applied to dry flies to help them float higher and longer before becoming water-logged. So, no one would think twice if dry fly flotant was applied. Agent Van Kampen, do you know if the FBI lab checked the dry fly flotant in Edgar's vest?"

Before Janet could answer, Gamby chimed in. "Look, Parker, you don't have to treat me like I'm a beginner when it comes to fly-fishing. I know about dry flies and fly flotant. Nice theory you have, but where is the proof?"

Parker could see that Hal Gamby was trying to discredit his theory without seeming to criticize Janet for even entertaining the theory. Parker continued. "Maybe, and I just thought of this now, the killer volunteered to put dry fly flotant on Edgar's fly. Edgar said sure … remember, he was used to being waited on by other people doing for him what he considered himself too important to do … and this could be how the killer switched the flies."

Again, Gamby broke in before Janet could say anything. "Sorry, Parker. I remember the hook on Hickson's fly being gold colored. This has been interesting table conversation, but you lose. You have been spending too much time dreaming about wild theories."

It was obvious that Gamby and Parker weren't going to agree on anything. Janet finally said, "To tell you the truth, I don't remember what color the hook is. I never paid any attention. The fly rod and fly are still at the FBI lab. I will call the lab and ask them to look. In the meantime, let's order. I'm hungry."

Parker ordered the buffalo pot roast special and iced tea. Janet ordered the same. Hal Gamby, maybe to show his independence, ordered a BLT with coffee. After ordering, Janet called the FBI lab in Denver. She told whoever answered what she was seeking. After ending the call, she said that the person said it would take a few minutes to check on the color of the hook and she should expect a return call within fifteen minutes.

Their orders arrived, and they ate in relative silence. Parker could feel the tension build as they waited for the call from the FBI lab. The buffalo pot roast was everything Jim claimed it to be. Parker wondered why he didn't eat buffalo more. Probably the cost, he thought, although the health benefits along with the taste more than made up for the additional cost.

After what seemed a much longer time than it was, Janet's cell phone rang. She answered, identified herself, listened for no more than fifteen seconds, thanked the caller, and switched off the phone. Looking across the table at Parker, she said, "You may have hit a home run. The hook is steel colored."

Chapter Fifteen

When he heard Janet say the hook was steel colored, Parker knew they had the killer, or at least had the killer pinned down to one of the three men presidents. But which one? There was no direct evidence pointing to one over the other two. Any one of them could have switched flies just as easily as the others. He couldn't determine a motive for one to kill Edgar any more than he could for the other two. Somewhere, there had to be direct evidence linking one of the men presidents to the murder, but until that evidence was found, all three were equal suspects.

What about Bryson Haggerty? He owed him an apology, or did he? It struck him that the poison used by one of the men presidents could have been supplied by Haggerty. He could be an accomplice. No, an apology wouldn't be forthcoming, at least not yet.

As Janet, Hal Gamby, and Parker exited the Lodgepole Pine Grill, Janet told Parker she was going to contact the FBI agents who had first interviewed the three men presidents and tell them about the probability that the flies were switched. These interviews might trigger something in the minds of the agents that hadn't been considered when they had first interviewed the presidents. Hal Gamby said goodbye and left Janet and Parker standing together. "Mr. Williams, I hope that when this investigation is over, we can get to know each other better," she said. "In fact, I was hoping you would help me get the hang of fly-fishing."

Parker wasn't sure if he should discourage this relationship from becoming more personal or go with the flow. At least for the time being, he decided to go with the flow.

"I would like that as well," he replied, "and as far as helping you with the ins and outs of fly-fishing, we could do that any evening when you aren't working or early morning before you go to work. Either time is good because the insect hatches are the best at those times."

"Maybe we could do an evening and the next morning," she responded. "I could stay over instead of driving back to Bozeman."

He didn't know how to respond or if he should. Was she implying that she wanted to stay overnight with him? Divert this conversation quickly was something he needed to do immediately. "Agent Van Kampen, does the probability that the flies were switched mean I'm no longer a suspect, nor are Dick and Jim?"

She laughed. "It looks that way to me, although officially all three of you remain suspects until we have identified the killer. But I don't think you need to be concerned, nor do Mr. Wells or Mr. Hill. And, while we're at it, how about we drop the Agent Van Kampen and Mr. Williams, unless we're in an official setting. Janet works for me."

"Sounds great. Parker works for me. Janet, I have another possible piece of evidence that might help narrow our list of suspects. I didn't want to mention it in front of Gamby. I simply don't trust him."

"You mean you don't like him. As I told you before, I don't like him either, but I'm stuck with him. Tell me what you are talking about."

He told her his second theory. "The word *strong* on the note, do you remember if it was capitalized?"

"No, I don't remember. Why do you ask?"

"If the word *strong* happened to be capitalized, it might indicate it doesn't refer to strength, but to the name of someone, an organization, business, or something other than meaning strength," said Parker. "How that links to anything else I'm not sure. But, it might."

She turned to him so he couldn't help looking at her. "Your last hunch proved correct, maybe this one will too. I'll call the evidence room at the office in Billings and have them check the note. I'll call you when I hear from them."

After saying goodbye, he walked to the fly shop with thoughts whirling around in his head. The hook was steel colored. Certainly, this meant that one of the three men presidents had switched flies with Edgar. The word *strong*, if it was capitalized, what could be done with that? There must be thousands of proper names with "Strong" being part of the name. Would there be a connection between the proper word *Strong* and the University of Colorado Health Sciences Center?

After entering the fly shop, he began to look through some promotional brochures for fly reels when his cell phone rang. The readout said FBI office, Billings.

"Hello, Parker Williams speaking."

"Hi, Parker, it's Janet. I called the three FBI agents that had interviewed the three men presidents and asked them to do another interview. This time, they are going to tell the presidents the flies were switched and watch for any reaction. Maybe one will know his number is up and give his guilt away by his reaction. Who knows, he might even confess."

"Wouldn't that be something," he replied. "When will you hear back from the agents?"

"They have to schedule the interviews first. It will probably take them a day to schedule the interview and conduct it. I should hear back shortly after that. I also contacted the evidence lab where the note is being held. I asked the agent in charge to check the note to see if the word *strong* is capitalized. I should hear from him within a few hours."

"Janet, has the fact that the flies were switched caused you to dismiss Bryson Haggerty as a suspect?"

"I haven't discounted him entirely, although I doubt he was the killer," she replied. "An accomplice maybe, but not the killer. He is an expert in poisons, and a poison was used to paralyze Edgar, so until the source of the poison is known and how it was obtained, I can't dismiss him, at least not yet."

"I agree," said Parker. "Haggerty could have supplied the poison to the killer."

"Is this another of your theories?" she joked.

"Not a theory, just a possibility. The killer had to obtain the poison from somewhere, and Haggerty could be the source."

"You're right. It is a possibility. Maybe I should obtain a search warrant for his cabin and take a look."

Placing his cell phone in its holder on his belt, he looked up to see Hal Gamby enter the fly shop. Gamby had a stern look on his face and walked directly toward Parker without acknowledging either Dick or Jim. "Listen, Parker. I don't know what you are trying to prove by being cozy with Agent Van Kampen, but I can see right through you. You aren't fooling me. I, for one, am not going to see this case screwed up by your messing around where you aren't wanted. Stay out of the way. The FBI asked for my help, not yours."

"Hal, I'm sorry you feel the way you do. I'm not trying to take your place or do anything to hinder you or Agent Van Kampen's investigation. I thought the information about the color of the hook was something she would want to know and check out. She seemed to welcome the information."

"Oh yeah, she welcomed the information all right, but I could care less how she felt. She shouldn't be allowing an amateur like you to be involved at all, and, if you ask me, she is being unprofessional and jeopardizing the case, and I intend to let her supervisors know about it." With that, he turned and walked out of the shop in a defiant manner.

"What was that all about?" asked Dick as he got up from his fly-tying bench and walked over to Parker.

"Gamby has his nose out of joint because he hasn't been able to crack the case of Edgar's murder," responded Parker. "He is accusing me of interfering in the FBI's investigation. I guess he can't stand it that Agent Van Kampen has listened to me."

Dick returned to his fly-tying bench while Parker picked up the brochure about new fly reels that he had been reading. Deciding to order several of the reels made by Sage in varying sizes, he was about to place a call to the sales representative for Sage when his cell phone rang. Checking the readout, it said the call was from an unknown cell phone number.

"Hello, this is Parker Williams."

A woman's voice answered. "Mr. Williams, my name is Amanda Martinez. I work in Professor Turner's office. He asked me to call you with some information you had requested. Professor Turner is attending a conference in Washington DC. He apologized for not calling you himself. He said you would understand."

"Ms. Martinez, thank you for calling. I asked Professor Turner to look into obtaining some information for me, and I'm pleased he didn't forget."

"I'm going to read verbatim from the note Professor Turner left me," she said. "I trust this will make sense to you. Here goes. 'Tell Parker to access the archives of the *Denver Post* and read a story written on April 25, 1978, about a burglary and killing at the Health Sciences Center. Then he should read another story, written May 3, 1978, about the capture of the suspects.' That's it. That's all he wrote. I hope this is the information you were seeking."

"This is more information than I had hoped for," responded Parker. "Thanks again for the call and please tell Professor Turner how much I appreciate his getting back to me."

Sensing this information might provide another piece in the puzzle, he told Dick he was going to the West Yellowstone Library. Dick said he was planning to be at the fly shop until closing. One of the many things Parker liked about Dick was that he didn't pry into your business. He merely said okay and continued to tie flies.

Chapter Sixteen

Parker had only a few minutes to spare if he wanted to make it to the library before it closed. He wanted to access the articles from the *Denver Post* that Carl had told him to read. The library was located next to the Madison Addition, a subdivision of homes on the northern edge of town, which had literally been carved from a lodgepole pine forest. Walking north on Yellowstone Avenue, he could see a buildup of thunderhead clouds over the Bridger Mountain range. If the bottoms of those clouds turned dark and the heads continued to boil up and grow in size, an early evening thunderstorm was a certainty. Such thunderstorms often included lightning, and that could mean forest fires. People in the Yellowstone area who were either living in the region in 1998 when the huge fires swept through Yellowstone National Park or heard stories about them were now much more wary of lightning than ever before.

A flash of lightning danced across the darkening sky, edges glowing pinkish, indicating that ice crystals were forming in the growing thunderheads. A far-off rumble of thunder resonated in the still evening air. How could anything so beautiful be so threatening at the same time? he wondered.

"Well, Parker Williams. I haven't seen you in quite some time. Where have you been keeping yourself?" He hoped he would avoid Cathy Marsman when he entered the library, but no such luck was his. Cathy was the director of the West Yellowstone Library, and he wanted to avoid her because she didn't hide her interest in establishing a relationship with him. The last thing he needed was another woman in his life. Cathy and he had sat next to each other at the recent library fundraising banquet, and that had been a mistake. She had taken a fancy to him, or so it seemed, and the night had gone painfully slow for him.

She had moved to West Yellowstone from Chicago, Illinois, with a fifteen-year-old son who was the star of the West Yellowstone High School basketball team. Even though he was only a sophomore, already the college scouts were attending games. It must have had something to do with his being 6'7" and growing. He was all feet and seemed to stumble over the lines on the court, or so it seemed to Parker, but height and quickness were everything in basketball, and he certainly had one of the two.

"Cathy, good to see you too," said Parker. "I've been much too busy lately with the fly shop and haven't had any time to come by the library to see all the improvements." If he were truthful, he would have told her that he was avoiding the library so he wouldn't have to talk with her. Cathy Marsman didn't raise any emotions in Parker. A nice woman, but that was as far as it went for him. "I'm wondering if I could use your library online account to access the archives of the *Denver Post*."

"For you, Parker, I'm sure we can," she responded.

Before he could object and say that he didn't want to take her away from her important work, she stood up and indicated he should follow her. They went downstairs and entered a small room with a computer, two chairs, and an old desk. Fortunately, from Parker's perspective, a small man, probably in his seventies, was seated at the desk. The presence of this man would curtail any extracurricular activities that Cathy might have contemplated if only she and Parker were in the room. She could be aggressive, and he wanted no part of it.

"Tom Watkins, meet Parker Williams," she said. Parker reached down, and they shook hands. A firm grip for an elderly man, thought Parker. "Tom is a volunteer whom we simply couldn't get along without."

Tom blushed as Cathy praised him. "Nice to meet you, Tom," said Parker.

"Did you say Parker Williams?" asked Tom. "The same Parker Williams who owns the Gold Medal Fly Shop?"

"One and the same," responded Parker.

"I purchased some flies tied by your employee, Dick Wells," said Tom. "Caught some nice browns down in Box Canyon with them. Those browns sure chewed those flies to bits. I'll have to stop by the shop and get some more."

"Tom is our expert in accessing the archives of newspapers," said Cathy. "If it's in an archive and that archive is accessible online, Tom will find it."

"Tom, you are just what I need," said Parker. "I'll tell you what. You find some articles from the *Denver Post* for me and you can have half a dozen flies compliments of the Gold Medal Fly Shop."

"It's a deal," responded Tom. "But I have to tell you, I think I got the better part of this deal. What articles do you want me to find?"

Parker wrote down for Tom what Carl Turner had passed on to him. "Tom, I'm hoping you can find an article from the April 25, 1978 issue of the *Denver Post* and another article from the May 3, 1978 issue. The April article was about a burglary and killing at the University of Colorado Health Sciences Center in Denver. The May article is about the burglars being apprehended. If there are additional articles about the burglary or the burglars, I would like to have those too."

"This might take me awhile," responded Tom. "No sense for you to wait around. I'll call you when I have something for you."

Thanking Tom, Parker said goodbye to Cathy Marsman and headed back to the fly shop. The sky was now very dark and the wind had picked up, sure signs that rain and maybe hail were on the way. Several bolts of lightning flashed across the sky, creating a patchwork of silver streaks against the dark background. Beautiful, but deadly, he thought, as he hustled down Yellowstone Avenue and entered the fly shop. As he did, his cell phone rang. The digital readout said FBI Office, Billings. It must be Janet Van Kampen calling, he thought.

"Hello, Janet, this is Parker."

"Hi, Parker. I received a call from the agents who interviewed the three men presidents. They said they confronted them with the switching of the flies. According to the agents, none showed any reaction other than to say that they didn't switch flies with anyone including Hickson. So, we aren't any further along with pinpointing the killer, if the killer is one of these three."

"Janet, I'm not surprised that none of the men presidents showed any reaction," responded Parker. "University and college presidents, in general, learn to hide their emotions and reactions. It comes from having to not personalize the criticisms that come every day. Faculty, in particular, are continually criticizing the president. On any given day, there is at least one faculty member who believes he or she would make a better president than you. After awhile, you learn to ignore the criticisms and keep moving ahead. Emotions are pushed aside in such an environment."

"A good point," she said. "I hadn't thought about that. Maybe the second piece of information I have for you will be better news. The agent at the evidence lab called back. The word *strong* was capitalized on the note. So, going on your theory, "strong" might be the name of either a person, an organization, a company, or something with the proper name Strong included. I'm having the FBI office in Denver contact the University of Colorado Health Sciences Center to inquire if a person with the last name Strong works there or had worked there. You have any other ideas or theories?"

He hesitated. Should he tell her about the *Denver Post* articles that Tom Watkins was searching to find for him? No, he decided he would let things ride for now. "Nope, no other ideas or theories."

"I will call you again when the Denver office lets me know what they find out at the Health Sciences Center. Talk to you later."

Chapter Seventeen
Friday
May 29

The telephone call from Tom Watkins that Parker received just before leaving the fly shop and the articles he picked up at the library had kept his mind going at a frantic pace throughout the night. Giving up on sleep, he had made his way into the kitchen, where he measured four tablespoons of Starbucks coffee, filled the reservoir in the four-cup coffeemaker with cold water, and pushed the "on" switch. Splashing some water on his face, he sat down at the kitchen table to read the articles again.

April 25, 1978 Teenager Gunned Down in Burglary at Health Sciences Center

An unidentified teenager was shot and killed Tuesday morning outside the south entrance of the University of Colorado Health Sciences Center by two apparent burglars.

The name of the teenager is being withheld pending notification of the next of kin.

Sgt. Burt Magneson of the Denver Police Department believes the teenager was in the wrong place at the wrong time. "The burglars were making their getaway, and the teenagers happened to be skateboarding on the escape route. One of the burglars apparently panicked when the escape route appeared to be blocked. He decided to shoot his way through the teenagers. At least this is the way we think the killing happened."

The burglars made off with Anthracoli 13XE, a super-virus under a national security clearance. The virus is highly toxic and kills instantly. It can be released into water supplies and could be used as a weapon in bioterrorism. The amount stolen from the Health Sciences Center is valued at $10 million.

Three other teenagers were skateboarding along with the teenager who was killed. None of the other teenagers were injured. Police are having the teenagers look through books of mug shots hoping that one or more of the burglars can be identified. The burglars made off in a white and green Ford van with Colorado license plates. Police are asking anyone who might have seen a white and green Ford van in the vicinity of the Health Sciences Center to contact Denver Police headquarters.

May 3, 1978 Burglars of Anthracoli 13XE from Health Sciences Center Apprehended

Killer of Teenager Close to Being Identified

Denver police believe the burglars of the Anthracoli 13XE from the University of Colorado Health Sciences Center have been apprehended. Police also believe the killer of Manuel Estrada will soon be identified. Estrada was the teenager gunned down by the burglars when he and his friends were skateboarding on the sidewalk outside the south entrance to the Health Sciences Center. Police have yet to release the name of the burglar they believe did the shooting. Two of the burglars have a history of petty theft. Police believe Max Bronson and Luther "Lefty" Harrison were the two who actually burglarized the Health Sciences Center. Police believe a third man, Daniel Strong, was the driver of the getaway vehicle, a white and green Ford van.

Police have yet to determine who was the mastermind behind the theft of the highly valuable toxic virus. With a value of $10 million, police have requested the assistance of the FBI due to the fact that national security may have been compromised if Anthracoli 13XE was allowed to fall into the hands of countries unfriendly to the United States.

Daniel Strong. Parker wondered if this was the person with the name Strong that was written on the note found in Edgar's room. This seemed to be a definite possibility since the capitalized word *Strong* and the words *Health Sciences Center* were both on the note. He was troubled why there were no more articles about the burglary and the killing of the teenager. Did Tom Watkins only search for the two articles Parker requested and not for more? What did a burglary many years ago have to do with Edgar Hickson? Had Edgar known something involving Daniel Strong or the burglary at the Health Sciences Center? Questions, questions, but no answers. No wonder he hadn't slept well.

Pouring a cup of coffee, he tried to determine what should be his next step. Should he call Janet Van Kampen and tell her what he had learned from Carl Turner, about the two articles Tom Watkins had found, and suggest she do a background search on Daniel Strong? Reaching for the telephone, he began to call her only to put the telephone down before finishing punching in her number. The two clues that had proven to be most useful hadn't come from Janet or via the FBI's investigation. Janet had only verified what he had suggested. In turn, he knew the clue about the color of the hook had come from Dick, and the clue about the word *strong* came from Beth. Instead of calling Janet, he decided to call Beth, since she seemed to have a sense about clues and how to find them. Maybe she would bring forth another theory or clue if he gave her the opportunity to do so.

Punching in Beth's telephone number, he realized one way to kill the developing relationship with her was to contact her only when he wanted her help with this investigation. Knowing he needed to ease into asking for her help, he decided to first ask her if she had lunch plans. Women could be strange about such things, and he didn't want to ruin the relationship.

After two rings, she answered with the official "Beth Richardson, assistant superintendent of Yellowstone National Park, how may I help you?"

He decided to answer in kind. "Dr. Parker Williams, proprietor of the Gold Medal Fly Shop. You may help me by agreeing to have lunch with me today at a place of your choosing." He hadn't used his academic title since he left the university. His PhD meant little outside of the academic community. He used it now as he thought she would find it amusing since she used her official title when answering.

"Dr. Williams, what a pleasant surprise. What a marvelous invitation. It so happens I am free for lunch. Did I hear correctly, the choice of a lunch spot is mine?" she asked.

"You heard correctly, Assistant Superintendent Richardson," he replied. "Your choice."

"Do you mind driving a little distance, Dr. Williams? I have most of the afternoon free, so I don't have to be back at any particular time."

"No, driving a little ways would be no problem at all. I too have the afternoon free. What do you have in mind?"

"That being the case, I choose the Gallatin Gateway Inn. I will drive to your shop and meet you at 11:30. Do you think we will need a reservation?"

"I don't think so, not this time of the year. But I will call anyway, just to be sure."

"Oh, Dr. Williams, I'm tired of wearing my Smokey the Bear uniform, so I shall wear something more in keeping with the season and the occasion. I hope that is okay with you."

He could almost feel electricity flowing over the telephone line. Lunch at the Gallatin Gateway Inn. She certainly had chosen a special place. Would there be flirtation to make the afternoon more than a social lunch? He needed to get control of himself before he did something foolish that he would regret. "Slow down, boy," he mumbled to himself.

He shaved, showered, and dressed in Dockers and a button-down, blue oxford shirt. Laughing as he used some aftershave cologne, he felt like a teenager who was going to have an ice-cream soda with the captain of the cheerleading squad.

He drove to the fly shop, where he found Laurie and Jim busily waiting on customers. "I'm going to be gone for most of the afternoon," he said. "Beth and I are going to drive to the Gallatin Gateway Inn for lunch. If something comes up, you can reach me via my cell phone."

"Wow, the Gallatin Gateway; must be a special lunch," Laurie said with a twinkle in her eye. "That is one nice place."

Concentrating on what brand of wading shoes he should order was difficult as his mind kept wandering with thoughts of Beth and how she had sounded on the telephone. His thoughts were interrupted by his cell phone ringing. The readout showed it was Beth calling.

"Beth, what's up?" he asked.

"Parker, I'm so sorry. There has been a serious accident at Yellowstone Canyon. A motor home and a van collided. I'm the closest ranger, and I'm on my way there now. I won't be able to make lunch. I'm really sorry. I'm wondering if you might be free this evening. We could have dinner instead of lunch if that would work for you."

"Beth, please don't feel badly. Nothing you can do about it. You are needed at that accident. Yes, I can do dinner tonight. What time would work for you?"

"Good, that makes me feel so much better. I'll come by the shop at 6. I'm really sorry, but thanks for understanding. See you this evening at 6."

He didn't know quite how to react. He had become so worked up thinking about lunch that he didn't know how he should feel now that he had several more hours to think about dinner and the evening. Plunging into work around the shop so that he would be distracted from thinking about dinner and the evening was what he needed to do.

The remainder of the morning was uneventful. He ordered the Sage fly reels, some Simms wading boots, Scientific Anglers fly lines, leaders, and tippet materials, and scheduled two large fishing outings with different groups as well as arranging for several individually guided fishing trips. When Jim and Laurie took their lunch break, he worked the register and waited on customers, many of whom asked about fishing conditions on the Firehole, Gibbon, Madison, Gallatin, and Henry's Fork rivers. Remembering to call the Gallatin Gateway Inn, he made a dinner reservation for 6:45, requesting a table by the fireplace.

Continuing to order merchandise and wait on customers at busy times made the afternoon go by quickly. Noticing it was nearly 5, he told Laurie and Dick to close the shop when they wanted. With just enough time to drive to his cabin, get dressed, and return to West Yellowstone to meet Beth, he was thankful he had done the dishes and given the cabin a basic cleaning. Something in his bones made him think that possibly Beth and he might be stopping at the cabin after dinner on the way back to West Yellowstone. Not that she would stay the night; no, this relationship had a ways to go before he would allow those thoughts to linger, even only momentarily, but he knew how women were often curious about "bachelor pads," and if she wanted to see the cabin—bachelor pad it wasn't—he wanted it to be presentable. He was grateful he had done a once-over on the bathroom sink, mirror, countertop, and stool since if they did stop at the cabin and she used the bathroom, he didn't want her to be embarrassed by it being unclean.

He had first seen the cabin during an afternoon of evaluating various places with Karen Black. He had contacted her while he was still in Sturbridge after he found her agency during a search of real-estate agency Web sites. Through several e-mail exchanges, he described the type of place he hoped to locate. Of utmost importance was living near a stream or river with trout while also reflecting the Yellowstone area without being too rustic. A primitive log cabin was fine for some people, but roughing it permanently wasn't his cup of tea. A modern, winterized place, with the capability of connecting to the world via Internet and e-mail, had been his preference.

A few months before he leased the cabin, it had undergone remodeling and upgrading. New triple-pane thermal wood windows, recessed lighting, and a large mossrock wood-burning fireplace in the great room brought openness and light into the main living area. One end of the great room housed the kitchen, complete with a wood-plank countertop island, double ovens, built-in microwave, and countertop range. A large master suite, powder room, and an office/study, with satellite Internet connection, comprised the remainder of the main floor. The upper level included two bedrooms with a full bath between them, as well as a den with built-in pine bookcases. A floor-to-ceiling picture window framed the forested hillsides and meadows adjacent to the park. A double slider from the master suite led to a deck from which Duck Creek could be viewed and the gurgling of it heard during the solitude of the evening and night. Almost every evening, the rising of trout, breaking the surface of the water in pursuit of flying mayfly insects, could be seen from the deck, a sight that never failed to start his casting arm twitching in anticipation of a forthcoming contest between fish and fisherman.

He drove back to West Yellowstone, parking in front of the shop. After only a few minutes, Beth's Chevy Tahoe turned the corner and parked next to him. His heart skipped a beat as he watched Beth walk over to his pickup. Her hair was back in a ponytail. Her makeup was ever so subtle, giving her face a glow that was penetrating. She wore a jean skirt with a silver Navajo belt buckle and a rose-colored light sweater, slightly scooped, and a light-blue accent scarf completed the wardrobe. Small silver hanging earrings glistened and were matched by a silver bracelet adorned with small pieces of turquoise. He thought she looked as beautiful and, at the same time, as wholesome as any cover girl on any women's fashion magazine.

"Hi, Dr. Williams, Assistant Superintendent Richardson reporting on time." As she said this, she broke into a big smile, which melted every fiber in Parker's body.

"Assistant Superintendent Richardson, you look dazzling," he said. "I've never seen your hair like that."

"Thank you, Dr. Williams. You don't look too bad yourself. But if we continue to stand here and compliment each other about our looks, we will never have that dinner you promised me."

"You're right," he replied. "We should be going, but only if we agree to drop the Dr. Williams and Assistant Superintendent Richardson stuff."

Talking and laughing about all sorts of personal life experiences, they drove Highway 91 north from West Yellowstone toward Bozeman. Passing the turnoff to his cabin, he pointed. "My cabin is about one mile down that road," he said.

"I hope I can see it sometime," she replied. "Seeing how you live can tell me some things about you that you probably wouldn't think to tell me."

His heart beat faster. Was she hinting she would like to see the cabin this evening? Better not presume too much, he thought.

He learned that her parents lived in Illinois, in a suburb of Chicago called Forest Park. She had been raised there with an older brother who had attended the University of Illinois, graduated with a degree in accounting, and was currently a CPA with his own accounting practice in Beloit, Wisconsin. Her family had taken a trip to Rocky Mountain National Park in Colorado when she was thirteen, and that trip convinced her she wanted to be a ranger in the national parks with an assignment in the West. She had attended Colorado State University in Fort Collins, Colorado, majoring in wildlife management. Her tuition had been paid by a Miss America scholarship awarded her when she was selected Miss Illinois her senior year in high school. After college, she had passed all the requirements for being a ranger with the National Park Service. She didn't pursue her goal for several years, but when she did, her first assignment was Capitol Reef National Park in Utah, followed by Big Bend National Park in Texas. She then was assigned to the Department of Interior in Washington DC. After what she described as three miserable years in Washington DC, she was assigned to Yellowstone National Park as assistant superintendent.

Parker shared with her his family background, his education, his various academic positions in higher education, and his university presidency. He made no mention of his brief marriage or the reason why he resigned his president's position. He couched it in terms referring to his desire to completely have a change in life and make a living while pursuing his passion, fly-fishing, and combining it with his interest in geology. The same way that he had been silent when she was telling him about her life, she remained quiet while she listened to his stories without asking questions.

They arrived at the Gallatin Gateway Inn a few minutes before 6:45. A table had been reserved adjacent to the fireplace. He was aware all eyes were on them—more accurately, on Beth—as they walked through the large dining room to their table. As he pulled the chair out for her, she smiled. "A man with manners. Doesn't happen too often anymore." The sparkle in her eyes told him she enjoyed it.

Originally built by the Chicago, Milwaukee, and St. Paul Railroad as a destination summer resort for visitors coming to Yellowstone National Park, the Gallatin Gateway Inn still maintained its grandeur. Original craftsmanship was on display in the Polynesian mahogany woodwork, carved beams, high arched windows, thirty-foot ceilings, and exquisite chandeliers. A great hall adjacent to the dining room boasted hand-painted large beams in a Spanish motif. A massive fireplace from floor to ceiling dominated the west wall of the great room. Several French doors opened onto a screen patio from which the Bridger Mountains were visible. On the south end of the great room was a spiral staircase bringing visitors to second-floor guest rooms.

They shared an appetizer of roasted mussels. She ordered roast pheasant, he the pork porterhouse. She chose the redskin mashed potatoes while he selected the cheesy crab au gratin stuffed baked potato. Both entrees included an assortment of vegetables. A basket of freshly baked breads and rolls accompanied the dinner. They shared a bottle of German wine. The food and service were superb.

He couldn't remember a time when he had enjoyed being with a woman over dinner and conversation as much as he did with Beth.

Maybe it was the combination of the atmosphere of the dining room, quality of the food, softness of the lighting, and the background music that did it. In truth, he knew it was Beth that made it so enjoyable. There was none of the gamesmanship or competition that marked so many of the relationships between the sexes these days. She didn't try to impress him, but impress him she did. Genuine, good conversationalist; sure of herself; conscious of her beauty without flaunting it—he found all these attributes irresistible.

When the waitress asked if they wished to order dessert, Beth said she preferred to pass and wanted instead to have a cup of coffee at his cabin. "Great idea. I'm not sure I have room for dessert anyway," he said. Asking for the check, he paid with his Mileage Plus Visa joking that at this rate, he would accumulate enough miles by using his credit card to fly around the world.

She took his hand as they walked to the pickup, and he opened the passenger door for her. She turned to him and kissed him on the cheek. "Thanks for a wonderful dinner. The conversation wasn't all that bad either," she joked as she slid into the seat. He shut the door and walked slowly around the back of the pickup, giving himself time to contemplate what had just taken place.

Chapter Eighteen

The sun was setting as Beth and Parker drove from the Gallatin Gateway Inn to his cabin. Shadows danced along the pine-covered hillsides as differing shades of pink and purple moved across the rocks and mountaintops like silent carriers of color. The Gallatin River glistened with the evening rays of light like a silver ribbon.

After several minutes of silence, she asked, "What has been happening with the Edgar Hickson murder investigation? I've been so busy with things around the Old Faithful complex that I've lost track of what's happened the last two days."

Parker was glad she brought up the investigation. Now she wouldn't think the dinner had only been a means to this end. "Do you wish to hear the three-minute version or the fifteen-minute version?" he asked.

"Tell me everything," she responded. "I want to especially know what you have been doing related to the case and if you think the killer will be identified soon."

He told her about Dick remembering he had used gold-colored barbless hooks for three of the flies and steel-colored barbed hooks for the other three flies. He described the probable switching of Edgar's fly. Complimenting her for her suggestion that the word *strong* had been capitalized, he told her the suggestion had turned out to be true. He described contacting Carl Turner at the University of Colorado Health Sciences Center.

"Beth, do you know Tom Watkins?" he asked. "He is a volunteer with the library who helps in the archives area."

"Yes, I know Tom," she responded. "A friendly guy. He certainly acts much younger than his age. I hope I'm that with it when I get to be his age."

"I asked Tom to access the archives of the *Denver Post* and find two articles about a burglary and killing of a teenager at the Health Sciences Center in 1978. Tom found the articles, and I have them at the cabin. What is strange, at least I think it's strange, is that the story goes cold after the second article, or at least it appears that way. No subsequent articles, not even about who the killer was or what sentence was given by the court. I find that strange."

"That is strange," said Beth. "I suspect the killing of a teenager was high profile, and for the media to say nothing about who the killer was, doesn't make sense. Is there anything else?"

"Agent Van Kampen had FBI agents interview each of the men presidents and confront each with the switching of the flies. She said none of them showed any reaction. She is also having a search of records of the Health Sciences Center to determine if someone with the last name of Strong works there or had worked there. In particular, I want to see if the name of Daniel Strong surfaces in the search.

"Who is Daniel Strong?" she asked.

"When you read the articles, you will see that he was the driver of the van used by the burglars to make their escape from the Health Sciences Center," he replied.

Parking in front of his cabin, he noticed the sun had not yet set but was behind the mountains, causing the western sky to glow orange and providing birds an excuse to give their end-of-the-day serenade while the croaking of the frogs along the bank of Duck Creek provided a background serenade all its own. "I don't think I'll ever tire of the sunsets around here," she said. "And look at the moon rising in the east; what a gorgeous combination. You know, they say that a full moon can make a person do things they normally wouldn't do."

Taking his hand as they walked up the path to the front door, he hoped she didn't hear his keys rattling together from the nervous shaking of his other hand, especially as he opened the door and stepped aside for her to enter. Following her and flipping on the switch controlling the two floor lamps, he stood with her in the middle of the room as she surveyed the surroundings. Smiling, she turned to him and said, "Just what I expected. A man's place and the place of a man I like."

Walking into the kitchen, he flipped the light switch. He took the Starbucks coffee from the cabinet over the counter and filled the coffeemaker with cold water. He flipped the switch to "on." "Do you take anything in your coffee?" he asked.

"Depends on how strong you make it." Her response was muffled, indicating she had entered the bathroom. Thank goodness, it's clean, he thought.

He could smell the coffee brewing. Walking into the kitchen, she sat down at the table and with a broad, captivating smile asked, "Is this when we talk about our hopes and dreams, or is that conversation reserved for tomorrow night?"

Hopes and dreams were not what he wanted to talk about with her, at least not while the investigation of Edgar's murder was unsolved. He wanted to know her thoughts about the investigation, especially if she had another theory. "If we talk about those," he said, "we'll probably be here all night."

"Are you hinting that you want me to stay the night?" she asked. "I'll have you know that I didn't bring my toothbrush or my nightgown, so I can't stay the night unless you keep spares around here." All the time she was saying this, her eyes were twinkling, and that captivating smile was again on her face.

He felt flustered. He must have turned red because she laughed again, reached across the table to grasp his hand, and said, "The coffee is ready; how about pouring me a cup?"

Thank goodness for the break, he thought. How she could traumatize him with her smile, her eyes, and her words. Did she want him to ask her to stay the night? Was it a harmless gesture on her part? Did he want her to stay the night? What did he want? He wasn't sure.

He poured her a cup of coffee and then one for himself. He watched as she sipped it. "Perfect, just the way I like it," she said.

"Good. You don't mind if I use a little half-and-half, do you?" he asked.

"Of course not," she responded. "If you want to spoil your coffee, go right ahead."

Opening the refrigerator, he took out a carton of half-and-half and poured some into his cup. Returning to the table, he noticed she was deep in thought. Not wanting to disturb her thoughts, he remained silent. Breaking the silence, she said, "I'd like to read those two articles from the *Denver Post*."

"Sure, let me get them," he said. He went into his bedroom and found the articles on the nightstand. "Here you are." He remained silent while she read them.

"I was thinking about what you told me about the articles stopping after only these two," she said. "It is very unusual in the newspaper business to not have at least one more article where the identity of the killer is published, and the fate of the killer and the burglars is known. One of my uncles worked for the *Chicago Tribune*. He always said that leaving a story where this one was left hanging was only done for particular reasons, usually via an order by the law enforcement authorities."

"You know, Beth, I did think about that myself," he said. "The killing of a teenager and the theft of such a highly valued substance as that stuff was would certainly warrant at least one follow-up story. Certainly, the burglars being apprehended and the killer identified would merit at least one story."

"It is like the police didn't want the public to know anything more about the situation," she said. "Kind of like what happens when national security is involved."

"Maybe Tom Watkins didn't search for subsequent articles, articles about the trial, convictions, whether the Anthracoli 13XE was ever recovered, and things like that," he replied. "I only identified these two articles, although I did ask him to look for additional ones. Maybe there are more, and he didn't search for them because it was getting late or he didn't feel like searching."

She remained silent. Sensing she was mulling something over in her mind, he too remained silent. "Let me think about this for a minute," she said as she took her coffee cup and walked onto the deck. The moonlight was such that she was silhouetted against the sky. Her profile struck him as being like a statue of a goddess. She turned and walked back into the room. "Are you interested in hearing a theory about what might have gone on to halt any subsequent news articles, assuming there aren't any more?" she asked.

"Sure," he responded. "Your last theory proved to be right on, so maybe you'll bat two for two."

"Okay, a little background first. When I was working in the Interior Department in Washington DC, there was a case involving the burglary of some valuable historical documents from the National Archives."

"You mean the big building on Constitution Avenue where the Declaration of Independence and the Bill of Rights are housed?" he asked.

"Yes, that building," she responded. "You can imagine the outcry and the embarrassment for the Interior Department if this had become known to the public. Interior Department officials were desperate to get the documents back. They also wanted to apprehend the masterminds behind the burglary. You see, the masterminds had hired some professional burglars to do the theft and paid them well for their effort."

"In other words, the big guys hid behind the little guys," he replied.

"Exactly. And the little guys were found after a few days. But remember, the Interior Department wanted the big guys. So, what do you think was done to get the big guys?"

"Well, in the movies, the little guys are pressured to tell who the big guys are or they are bribed," he responded.

"Not bad. A good guess. The little guys were bribed. But here's what has tweaked my theory about why the articles stopped about the burglary and killing of the teenager outside the Health Sciences Center. The little guys who pulled the burglary at the National Archives knew they could get more than money, so they held out for more."

"Well, Joe Q. Public doesn't like to entertain this notion, but I suppose if they were holding out, the government could have ordered they be tortured in order to extract the information," he said. "I'm sure it wouldn't be the first time the U.S. government tortured prisoners to obtain information."

"No, torture wasn't used, at least not this time," she responded. "I think the Secretary of the Interior couldn't face having torture on his conscience. Other than torture, any other guesses?"

"If torture wasn't used to obtain information and neither was money, what else could be attractive enough to make the little guys rat on the big guys," he wondered out loud. Then it hit him. "I suppose the government could excuse them from any sentencing for their crimes, some type of probation," he said.

"Not bad," she replied. "You're getting better. As I remember, there were some officials in the Interior Department that wanted to cancel the sentence and place the burglars on probation. But remember, valuable historic documents were involved. Many more officials demanded that justice be administered. Have you ever heard of the Federal Witness Protection Program?"

"Sure. Isn't that where a person receives an entirely new identity, settles in a new location, has a history manufactured with birth certificate, social security number, educational history, and all the other necessary changes, all in exchange for information the government wants?"

"Yes, that's about it," she responded. "In this case, the U.S. government offered one of the burglars protection under the Federal Witness Protection Program in exchange for the names of the masterminds. The burglar jumped at the offer. The government had the people it wanted."

Parker looked at her. This time he saw more than beauty. He saw a keen mind able to dissect options and possibilities. He began to see the outline of her theory. "So, you're thinking that if there were no more articles, this burglary and killing at the Health Sciences Center might have been handled in much the same way as the burglary at the National Archives. You think that one or more of the burglars went into the Federal Witness Protection Program in exchange for information about the big guys that planned the burglary and obtained that virus stuff."

"You really are getting good at this," she said. "That is another thing I like about you. You are quick to size things up. I know you are still trying to size me up, so you're not so quick with everything, but you've got the picture as far as my theory goes."

Her eyes were sparkling as she talked. She was both teasing and flirting at the same time, and he found it terribly enticing. "You're right, Beth, I can't figure you out. But right now I don't want to talk about that. I want to stick with your theory. If I'm following your line of thought, you're thinking Daniel Strong might be the burglar who went into the Federal Witness Protection Program."

"Either he or the burglar that didn't shoot the teenager. The burglar that killed the kid would be the last choice of the government. He would be approached by the government only if the other two turned the offer down. Again, you're quick"—she smiled and batted her eyelashes, not even trying to hide her flirtatious mood—"I agree it was probably Daniel Strong. He was the driver of the getaway vehicle and thus had nothing to do with the shooting."

"So, if Strong took the witness protection route, he would have a new identity," responded Parker. "You don't suppose that Daniel Strong became Edgar Hickson, and the masterminds behind the burglary at the Health Sciences Center tracked him down and made him pay for ratting on them?"

"I don't like disagreeing with you," she replied, "especially since we are trying to figure out what we want our relationship to be, but I think rather than Edgar Hickson being Daniel Strong, one of the men presidents is Daniel Strong. If I'm right, I think I know the motive one of them had for killing Edgar."

"Okay, Miss Sherlock Holmes, let's hear it."

"Edgar found out what I just said, except he knew which of the men presidents is Daniel Strong. Edgar was going to blab it and embarrass that person. This person knew he had to stop Edgar. So he killed him. He couldn't allow Edgar to ruin his reputation and his career."

Chapter Nineteen
Saturday
May 30

Brian Carlson was arrested on suspicion of murder six hours after Parker called Janet Van Kampen and told her about the two articles from the *Denver Post* linking Daniel Strong to the burglary of Anthracoli 13XE at the University of Colorado Health Sciences Center and the killing of Manual Estrada. Outlining the possibility that Daniel Strong had been given a new identity through the Federal Witness Protection Program, Parker described the theory that Daniel Strong and one of the men presidents were one in the same person.

Through confidential channels that would never be known outside the few people who have access to the records, Janet Van Kampen was notified by FBI headquarters in Washington DC that Brian Carlson and Daniel Strong were the same person. Confronted with the knowledge of his background as Daniel Strong and his changed identity, Brian Carlson confessed to FBI agents sent to his office. Further investigation found a small bottle of tetraodontoxin poison in a locked drawer of his desk. Subsequent investigation traced the purchase of the poison by Carlson from sources in Haiti who extracted tetraodontoxin from the ovaries of blowfish.

Janet Van Kampen had promised to provide Parker with as many of the details as permissible without jeopardizing the FBI's case against Brian Carlson or the ins and outs of the Federal Witness Protection Program. She told him she would be able to tell him how Brian Carlson said he committed the murder as soon as she cleared up a matter with her supervisor regarding Parker's involvement in the investigation. A complaint regarding Parker's interference and his so-called cozy treatment by her had been filed, and a meeting with her supervisor was scheduled later in the day to discuss the complaint. Parker had apologized for forgetting to tell her about his conversation with Hal Gamby and how Gamby had threatened to contact her supervisor.

"Don't worry," Janet said, "with the case solved, I doubt Gamby's complaint will go anywhere, especially when I advise my supervisor of the clues you provided. Without those clues, we might still be floundering around. The complaint is now more a formality than anything else."

"Janet, I'm relieved to hear that," he responded, "but I can't take the credit for any of the clues. Dick provided the clue about the switching of the flies, and Beth Richardson outlined the theories about the word *strong* being capitalized and Daniel Strong entering the Federal Witness Protection Program and assuming the identify of one of the men presidents."

"Parker, it seems that you and Beth Richardson have been spending time together since you obviously had to be discussing the investigation with her. Are you and she an item?" asked Janet.

"I don't know what you mean by an item, Janet, but if you are asking if we are friends, the answer is yes. But it isn't anything more than that. She is a friend like you are a friend."

"I'm glad to hear that," she responded. "I have nothing against Beth, but I was hoping you and I could get together, perhaps for that fly-fishing instruction we talked about."

****

Knowing the best way to clear his head and wind down from the pressures of the week was to lose himself in fly-fishing, Parker drove to Mesa Falls on the Henry's Fork River in Idaho, about twenty-five miles from West Yellowstone. While he had had better times on the Henry's Fork in terms of the number and size of the trout he caught and released, he did manage to catch and release several rainbow and brown trout in the fourteen-to-seventeen-inch range. More importantly, it contributed to giving him a feeling of exhaustion, which led to his taking a nap in the front seat of his pickup.

He headed back to his cabin around 3:30, allowing plenty of time to pick up the cabin, shower, shave, dress, and drive back to West Yellowstone to meet Beth. On the way to his cabin, he stopped at a roadside fruit stand and purchased fresh strawberries. He wanted to be ready with some refreshments in case Beth wanted to spend some time at the cabin after the theater.

As he was dressing, Janet Van Kampen called. She hoped he would understand that some of the details regarding the apprehension of the masterminds behind the burglary of the Anthracoli 13XE were still classified. Most of the information regarding the Federal Witness Protection Program was also classified. "Here is what I learned about Brian Carlson's motive for killing Hickson," she said. "He told the FBI agents that Edgar had found out about Brian being Daniel Strong and also that Carlson, I mean Strong, had been involved in the burglary at the University of Colorado Health Sciences Center. Carlson said he had been given $100,000 and a new identity by the Feds in exchange for the names of the masterminds behind the burglary. The masterminds were going to sell the Anthracoli 13XE to a Russian operative who was a known KGB official. What Russia wanted with the stuff is classified, but I guess they were going to use it to blackmail some members of NATO."

Parker listened as she continued.

"Edgar threatened Carlson with exposure. Carlson knew this would ruin his career and bring disgrace to his family. It seems that Daniel Strong turned over a new leaf when he became Brian Carlson. He enrolled in college and eventually earned a PhD in chemistry from the University of Indiana. He held a faculty position in the chemistry department at the University of Wisconsin and was chairman of the department for several years. He then became dean of the College of Arts and Sciences at the University of Iowa, followed by being the Vice President for Academic Affairs at the University of South Dakota. He met Edgar at one of the conferences involving university and college presidents after he became a president."

"Janet, did Carlson say how he administered the poison?"

"We know that Edgar died from drowning, although he was first paralyzed from the poison," she responded. "Tetraodontoxin is fast acting and causes both respiratory and nervous system paralysis. Nasty stuff. Edgar never knew what hit him, I suspect. Being paralyzed, he collapsed into the river and drowned. Being a fly-fisherman, you should be able to answer your own question about how the poison was administered, at least I've been told that all fly-fishers do the same thing when they tie the fly to the fly line, or do you call it tippet?"

"I tie the fly to the tippet using an enhanced clinch knot. It maintains the strength of the tippet," he said.

"Do you do anything with the knot before you pull it tight?" she asked.

"Sure, I wet the tippet with my saliva," he replied. "That way the strength of the knot isn't compromised."

"Aha, you got it," she said. "When Edgar tied the Royal Wulff fly coated with the tetraodontoxin to his tippet, he ran the tippet through his mouth. He would have touched the fly with his lips or tongue. That was enough for him to ingest some of the tetraodontoxin. A little bit of that stuff goes a long way. Paralysis ensued immediately."

Parker pictured Edgar tying the Royal Wulff fly to the tippet and wetting down the tippet and fly with his saliva before pulling the knot tight.

"Carlson stated that he put the poison into a Gurky's Fly Flotant container. When Edgar was outside the van last Saturday talking with someone, Carlson said he switched his Royal Wulff fly with Edgar's after putting some tetraodontoxin on the fly, which he switched for Edgar's original fly. Nobody questioned what he was doing, if they even saw him do it, since putting dry fly flotant on a fly, I'm told, is common. Is that true?" she asked.

"Sure is," responded Parker. "All of us do it when we use a dry fly. Janet, did he say anything to the FBI agents about noticing that Edgar's original Royal Wulff fly was tied on a gold-colored barbless hook while his fly was tied using a steel-colored barbed hook? I would think if he had noticed, he would have worried that Edgar would have noticed the switch."

"The agents didn't report that he realized the hooks were different colors. I will have to read the transcript of the confession to see if they thought it not important enough to tell me."

"But there's more," she said. "Carlson said his original plan was to let Edgar's body stay in the river. He knew Edgar had drowned, so keeping the body in the water made sense. However, he knew that a floating body, with so many people fishing on opening day, would be spotted immediately. He needed time. He had to rejoin the fishing group and get back to the Cutthroat Conference Center. Thinking that time would provide him with an alibi, he dragged the body into the trees along the bank of the river where you found it."

"What about Edgar's fly rod?" Parker asked. "If Carlson had found it, he could have cut off the Royal Wulff fly from the end of the tippet. Without the clue of switching flies, he might still be a free man."

"Carlson said he didn't realize that Edgar had dropped his fly rod into the water. He realized it only when he was back at the Yellowstone Conference Center. He thought about renting a car and returning to the Firehole River to look for it, but he ruled that out as being too risky. He had been watching Edgar from the trees into which he later dragged the body. He saw Edgar stumble and collapse into the river. He immediately waded out into the river and pushed Edgar's head under the water. In his haste to get Edgar's body from the water and into the trees, he forgot about Edgar's fly rod. His haste proved to be his undoing. Your finding Edgar's fly rod was a huge break in the case, although none of us realized it at the time."

She assured him that if more details of the case became known to her, she would pass them along. She again thanked him for his help. "By the way, Hal Gamby won't be helping me or anyone else within the FBI again. In fact, I hear that Sheriff Larson is reassigning him to traffic-control duty."

Looking at his watch, Parker realized he had only enough time to drive to West Yellowstone to meet Beth. As he drove, he couldn't help feeling sorry for Brian Carlson or Daniel Strong, or whatever name you preferred. Being threatened by an arrogant and pompous man like Edgar Hickson would drive anyone to drastic action. But, murder was going too far. And poor Edgar, had he not threatened Carlson, he would still be alive today.

Stunning and *captivating* were the words he thought as he met Beth. During *Annie Get Your Gun*, they laughed, hummed along with the music, ate popcorn during intermission, and held hands throughout the second half of the production.

After the production, she leaned into him as they walked to his pickup.

"On the drive to your cabin, I want to hear about the outcome of the Edgar Hickson murder case," she said. "Once we get to your cabin, no more talk about it. Remember, this is the evening when we talk about hopes and dreams."

****

He slipped his arm around her as they walked from the pickup to his cabin. Opening the door, she turned to him with her eyes sparkling and a charming smile. "Oh yes," she said, "in case we talk until quite late, I did bring my toothbrush. But I forgot my nightgown. You do have a T-shirt I can borrow, don't you?"

About The Author

Raymond Kieft possesses a doctorate in mathematics and has held faculty appointments in several colleges. He also served as the president of two colleges and as interim president of a third. He provides consulting services to colleges, universities, K-12 schools, and other educational organizations in-between being a fly-fishing guide and writing mystery novels. A member of The Federation of Fly-Fishers, Trout Unlimited, and the Greater Yellowstone Coalition, he has been an avid fly-fisherman for twenty-five years, annually fly-fishing in the Yellowstone region of Wyoming and Montana. He lives with his wife Sandy adjacent to Rocky Mountain National Park in Estes Park, Colorado.

CPSIA information can be obtained at www.ICGtesting.com
Printed in the USA
LVOW061748010512

279900LV00001B/282/A

9 781418 464561